Arnolfini

ART *Mysteries*

2

Rich
DiSILVIO

Cover art and interior illustrations © Rich DiSilvio. *Leda and the
Swan* close-up on cover (painted by Il Sodoma) is by Alvesgaspar.
Roman Reveries painting by fictional character Ricardo Cafaldo by
Rich DiSilvio. Gravensteen Castle photo by Marc Ryckaert,
colorized by Rich DiSilvio. Fort Mutzig photo by Thomas-Bresson.
Chapel Saint Hubert by Claudev8. Liszt Academy photo by Thaler
Tamas. Bedroom of Virginia Poe by Midnightdreary. Cathedral
Building photo by Sanfranman59. Tribune Tower photo by
Chris6d. Milan Cathedral and Galleria photo by © Steffen
Schmitz. Galleria Vittorio Emanuele II by © C. Messier. Photos of
historical figures and artwork of famous artists are in the public
domain, courtesy of Wikipedia.

Author's Website: www.richdisilvio.com

- - - - - - - - - - - - - - - - - -

Names: DiSilvio, Rich
Title: Arnolfini Art Mysteries 2
Description: NY, USA: DV Books, an imprint of Digital Vista, inc.
Identifiers: ISBN 978-1-950052-06-6 (paperback) |
ISBN 978-1-950052-05-9 (eBook)
Subjects: Art Crimes | Mysteries, Thrillers | Private Investigator
| Artists, Composers | Detective Stories | Short Stories
Illustrations/Photos: 37

THE AUTHOR

Rich DiSilvio is a multi-award-winning author of mysteries/thrillers, historical fiction, Sci-Fi/fantasy, nonfiction, and children's books. He has also written articles and commentaries for magazines and online resources. His passion for history, art, music, and architecture has yielded contributions in each discipline in his professional careers.

DiSilvio's work in the entertainment industry includes projects for documentaries, including James Cameron's *The Lost Tomb of Jesus*, *Killing Hitler*, *The War Zone* series, *Return to Kirkuk*, *Operation Valkyrie*, and cable TV shows and films such as *Tracey Ullman's State of the Union*, *Celebrity Mole*, *Blood Ties*, *Monty Python: Almost the Truth*, and many others.

He has written commentaries on the great composers (including the Franz Liszt Site), and conceived and designed the *Pantheon of Composers* porcelain collection for the Metropolitan Opera, which also retailed throughout the USA and Europe.

His artwork and new media projects have graced the album covers and animated advertisements for numerous super-groups and celebrities, including, Pink Floyd, Yes, The Moody Blues, Cher, Madonna, Jay-Z, Willie Nelson, Miles Davis, the Rolling Stones, Jewel, Alice Cooper, Queen, Black Sabbath, and many more.

As a software designer/developer, Rich pioneered the first interactive CD-ROM for educating staff and parents about Applied Behavioral Analysis (ABA) for training individuals with autism.

Rich lives in New York with his wife and has four children.

Contents

LEONARDO'S LEDA

Armand Arnolfini, and his bride-to-be, Andrea St. John, stood at the altar in Saint Bavo Cathedral in Ghent, Belgium, as Bishop Van Peteghem orchestrated a touching service.

In the first row of pews, Andrea's parents looked on with warm smiles of affection while Armand's father, Sergio, gazed at his tall and handsome son with a deep sense of love and pride. The six years Armand had lived as a widower, consumed in his work, had concerned Sergio, hoping for the day when Armand would meet another woman to get on with his life *and* procreate. The mere thought that the Arnolfini bloodline might fade away into oblivion had weighed heavily on him, being rather obsessed with the family's prominent history.

Upon the conclusion of the ceremony, the bride and groom, each decked out to perfection, turned and walked down the aisle. As they did, they nodded with smiles at their friends who had made the trek to Belgium, including Bernard Higley, Clara Vandermeer, Anton Platzer and Andrea's circle of friends, many of whom were also in the arts or museum industry. As the entourage followed the bride and groom several blocks to the reception, they appeared like a who's who of the art world.

To Andrea and their guests' surprise, Armand had utilized his father's connection to the curator of the Gravensteen Castle, whereby renting out the historic edifice for the evening's festivities. Armand had been waiting for this moment to enjoy the shocked look on their faces, knowing that the medieval castle provided a fitting ambiance for his darling new bride and their cadre of culture vultures.

Andrea's eyes lit up as she turned and hugged Armand. She had been duped into thinking the reception would be held at a nearby hall, but Armand's touching gift moved her deeply. Unable to contain her tears of joy, Andrea wiped away the rivulets, leaned in for an ardent kiss, then said, "You precious bum, now my makeup will be ruined before the night even begins."

Armand chuckled, as he wiped away a tiny smudge off her rosy cheeks. "Your makeup is fine, dear. You look magnificent."

Just then, two knights, decked out in authentic armor, approached the couple: One held a pole with a colorfully embroidered banner, designed by Armand, featuring a coat of arms with their initials, while the other knight held two crowns, also designed by Armand, each meticulously crafted of equal size and weight, for as Armand said, to avoid any trouble.

As Andrea turned and looked on with amazement, the knight placed the crowns on their heads, then both knights escorted the royal couple into the castle.

By all accounts, the reception was a spectacular affair, with fresh flowers arranged in vases on each table, and walls personally decorated by Armand and his father, with framed reproductions by a variety of medieval and Renaissance masters. Meanwhile, during the cocktail hour, a thirty-piece orchestra played Armand's favorite Classical tunes, including Liszt's *Liebestraume*, an excerpt from

Sibelius' *Fifth Symphony*, and an assortment of arias from Puccini's operas.

Afterwards, Armand escorted his bride and guests through the castle with torches and candles for authenticity. Traversing the labyrinth of tall corridors with barrel-vaulted ceilings and stone columns, they all were captivated by the medieval atmosphere and the castle's ancient history, including its sordid past as they descended down a flight of narrow stairs and entered the torture chamber. As they entered the dark room, the flickering waves of candlelight danced on the stonewalls and ceiling, as they gazed upon all the morbid tools of death. Included in the lineup were a guillotine, stretching racks, and various tools of torture mounted on the walls.

As the guests crowded around the macabre machines, Armand jested with the intonation of a king, "Hear me well, my most dear and loyal subjects. Whosoever dares to harm my beautiful queen shall be subjected to the tools of my trade!" As the guests laughed, he continued, "So spread thy words of warning to all within our grand kingdom." Reverting to his own voice, he added, "But now, it's time to eat!"

With another round of laughter, the entourage followed Armand and Andrea up a series of stairs and entered the main dining hall. A live band kicked off an evening filled with love songs ranging from Frank Sinatra, Perry Como, and Barbra Streisand to the more rocking tunes of the Beatles, Four Seasons, Moody Blues, and even a thunderous love song that grabbed everyone's attention— *Sabbra Cadabra*!

As to be expected, an exceptional gourmet menu of French and Italian dishes, from *Veal Duxelles* to *zuppa di pesce*, complimented a truly exquisite night, topped off by an equally impressive Venetian hour with a broad selection of liqueurs, gelato, cannolis, Italian cheese cake, French pastries, and of course Armand's favorite—tiramisu.

Several hours later, when the festivities ended, the married couple bid their family and friends good-bye, as Armand thanked and kissed his mother-in-law, Marie, who was the second-to-last person to leave. He then turned toward his father.

The two embraced, as Sergio said, "Armand, I'm so happy for you and Andrea. You make an extraordinary couple, and that's not just because I'm your father."

Armand nodded warmly with appreciation, as Sergio continued, "Now listen, I know you plan on going to Lake Como and then touring the scenic beauties of the Dolomites in northern Italy, but I have a surprise for you, one I just learned of before I left home." Excitedly, he punched the palm of his left hand. "And boy, is it a doozy!" His eyes glistened as he went on, "I've been fighting to keep it a secret all the while I've been here, Armand, and you know how hard it is for *me* to keep secrets, especially from you."

Armand's warm smile morphed into a suspicious smirk. He could always sense when his father had something up his artistic sleeve that would divert his attention and consume him. "Papa, I can see it in your eyes. No! Do you hear me? No way! Don't do this."

Just then, Andrea walked up alongside her groom, as he continued, "I'm going on my honeymoon with Andrea, Pop, so I'm not interested in starting any new cases."

"But, son, wait until you hear what I—"

"Dad," Andrea interjected, as she reached over and grasped Sergio's hand warmly. "You know Armand will oblige you once we return from our honeymoon. So, I'm sure whatever it is can wait two weeks."

Sergio glanced back and forth between Andrea's vibrant and innocent eyes and Armand's peeved and perceptive eyes.

Armand grasped Andrea's hand and started to walk her away, as he said, "She's right, Pop. We'll catch up when we return. I've waited six years for this moment."

As the loving couple started to exit the castle, they could hear Sergio's voice behind them say: "Very well, Armand. You've waited six years. But the world has waited *three hundred and sixty years* to see Leonardo's lost *Leda and the Swan.*"

Armand stopped dead in his tracks! His head spun around, as Andrea's followed suit. "Pop! Are you pulling my leg?" Armand demanded. "That would be a pretty awful thing to do on my wedding day."

Sergio shrugged and playfully gazed down at the castle's stone floor, littered with confetti by well wishers, then back up into his son's electrified eyes. "You know I'd never jest about something as monumental as a da Vinci, my son." He stuck his hands in his pockets, looked down again at the confetti, and softly kicked a few strands randomly with his foot. He looked back up. "But go ahead, you both have your honeymoon to go on, this miraculous lost masterpiece—by Western civilization's most revered and versatile genius—can surely wait. That is, *if* the trail doesn't dry up, of course."

Armand's lips twisted with a mixture of love and irritation: love, at how his father knew how to snag his attention, and irritation, at how this astounding news interfered with his amorous plans.

Meanwhile, Andrea's mind reeled with fascination, as her eyes bounced back and forth between father and son. She was madly in love with Armand and wanted desperately to spend two carefree weeks of utter bliss with her Italian stud in the Italian Alps, but she was also thrilled to now be a part of the prominent Arnolfini clan, a family that dealt with mega-titans of the art world. And who, by most accounts, sat at the apex of the Art World? *Leonardo da Vinci.*

Andrea had to speak. "So, Dad, just how viable is this lead?"

Armand's head jerked as he now looked at his bride. "Honey!? You know how much I love Leonardo, but I love *you* more. Are you seriously thinking about giving up on our honeymoon to chase down a painting, one that very well might not even be authentic? I'm sure two weeks won't make a difference."

Sergio smirked as he meticulously straightened out his tuxedo. "I thought I taught you better than that, Armand." In his well-seasoned and pedantic voice, the emeritus art professor added, "As I've always said to you and all my students, 'You must know *all* the details before making a decision.'"

Armand huffed as his eyes veered at his father. Before Sergio could say another word, Armand raised his hand. "Hold on! I know what you're going to say, Pops. I shouldn't think with my heart in matters such as this. So, tell me, what's so pressing about this lead that it can't wait two weeks?"

Sergio walked toward them, as they now all stood just outside the castle's stone-archway, several feet from the street. "Armand, before I left to come here I was contacted by Claude De Ville, a Frenchman who I had met briefly many years ago. He comes from a very affluent and powerful family with a rich network of friends, not necessarily *in* the art world, but with fellow titans in the financial industry and many industrialists, most of whom have rather impressive art collections."

Andrea looked on with growing interest while Armand pressed, "Well, Pops, that's all well and good, I'm glad Mr. De Ville is a rich Frenchman with connections, but what's his connection to Leonardo's lost *Leda and the Swan* and the big rush?"

Sergio motioned to the limousine he had ordered, which just then pulled up. "Why don't we speak about it in the limo on our way to the airport?"

"Pop!" Armand bellowed. "You must be kidding!?" His eyes glanced at the limo, then back at his father. "You mean to say you already arranged this coup? *Jeez*, are you still going to treat me like I'm twelve?"

Sergio smiled. "No, Armand, not twelve. But as you know, a son never grows older than his parents during their time together on Earth. So, yes, Armand, you are, and always will be, my one and only boy. And this lead is not something we should dilly-dally about."

As Sergio gently escorted Andrea to the limo, she gazed back at Armand with an enthusiastic grin and winked. "Come on, sweetheart. Listen to your father, this is a once in a lifetime adventure."

Armand shook his head, his mind reeling. He had invested the largest share of his life learning about and loving art and culture with a fervid passion, knowing well how critical it was to the upward climb of the human species. But with the devastating death of his first wife, whom he occasionally neglected due to work, he had learned a valuable lesson the hard way; namely, how precious the loved ones are in one's life. And now that he was graced with the beautiful gift of marriage once again, he wanted to set his priorities straight. Therefore, he just had to tell his headstrong father and beloved new wife that the paint and canvas of a priceless painting would *not* take precedence over the flesh and blood of the people he loved and cherished.

Yet, as he walked to the limousine, his eyes caught hold of Andrea's, who was now glowing with exhilaration as she sat in the back seat gazing up at him. Her stare was electrifying, just as *she* was to his very heart and soul, which now tingled with a sublime sensation, one that gave him pause. That Andrea would now accompany him on crime cases impacted his decision, which in this case allowed him to pursue lost artwork by perhaps Western civilization's most prized genius while having the honor and good fortune of being with the woman he loved, the woman who reawakened his heart and filled his universe with supreme bliss. How fortunate—he now thought, as he gazed at Andrea and his father—to be with the people he adored above all others and engaged in a career that he esteemed above all others. Suddenly, it all felt right.

With a satiated grin, Armand slipped contentedly into the back of the limo. The chauffeur closed the door behind him and hopped in the driver's seat. With a slight jerk, the car took off toward the airport.

Sergio reached into the liquor cabinet and pulled out a special bottle he had bought just for the occasion. With a smile, he poured each of them a glass of wine, which elicited a chuckle from his captive guests, as Andrea said, "Well, well, Da Vinci Chianti. You think of everything, don't you, Dad?"

Sergio winked. "Of course, my darling new daughter. As you know, we curators must orchestrate every detail." He gazed at the deep red liquid in his glass and gently swirled it around to aerate it. "For an inexpensive wine, the Sangiovese grapes of the Chianti region are quite flavorful."

Andrea clinked glasses with her new father-in-law and her new husband. "Then, here's to us. *Salute!*" she said with a warm gesture. "I couldn't be happier than I am right now."

As they each took a sip, Sergio lowered his glass and replied, "Well, hopefully we'll all be even happier once we land in France, so we can find Leonardo's lost *Leda*."

Armand practically choked on his wine. "What do you mean *France*? And *we*? Are you tagging along on this venture?" Armand had visions of turning this case into a dual endeavor, one filled with love *for* Leonardo's lost *Leda*, as well as making love *to* Andrea.

Sergio replied matter-of-factly, "Armand, of course I'm tagging along. *Monsieur* De Ville contacted *me*, yes? So, naturally, it's only proper that *I* accompany you to meet with him in Paris, so we all, with God's grace, may find and return this masterpiece."

Armand had to chuckle, as he shook his head, while Andrea raised her glass of wine once again. "The apple—or in this case, the grape—doesn't fall far, does it?"

As father and son laughed and clinked glasses with Andrea, the limo sped toward the airport, while Armand keenly noticed how his father never answered his question: *What was the rush?*

Landing at Charles de Gaulle Airport, the threesome hopped in a taxi and headed toward Claude De Ville's office, located on the outskirts of the heart of Paris. As they weaved through the city streets, they could see the Eiffel Tower standing majestically across the Seine, while well-dressed pedestrians walked the business sector of Paris. Turning down Rue Louis David, they arrived at their destination.

Mounted on the ornate, Mansard-roofed building was a large black plaque with gold letters that read "De Ville Financial Investments." As they entered, Armand noticed that the building engulfed almost the entire block.

Sergio approached the receptionist, as Armand and Andrea looked around the opulent lobby, decorated with an eclectic mix of rare artifacts and two original paintings by French masters, one by Gérôme and one by Fragonard. Sergio turned and waved eagerly, "Come, children! *Monsieur* De Ville will see us."

The mature newlyweds shook their heads and chuckled as they followed Sergio into De Ville's office. The spacious room featured an equally impressive array of fine art by several minor French artists, but most striking of all, were the framed portraits of De Ville's ancestors, each lined up behind Claude, all titans of the banking and financial industries. On Claude's lavish rosewood desk—with its intricate inlays, marble top, and 18 carat gold accents—stood a large, bronze statue of Napoleon.

As Claude approached them and Sergio made the introductions, Armand's eyes surveilled the office, eventually landing on the bronze statue. As he shook De Ville's soft, frail hand, he said, "I see you like Napoleon, and quite aptly located your office on Rue Louis David, Napoleon's favorite and personal artist."

Claude was tall; six-foot four with gray distinguished hair, and a lanky frame, one Armand deduced was prone to sitting and calculating interest rates and transaction fees to fleece his prey, rather than actively producing anything of true value, as De Ville smiled proudly and replied, "You are quite right, Mr. Arnolfini. Your keen sense of deduction is exactly why I reached out to your father. But..." he gazed admiringly at his prized statue. "I must confess, while many view Napoleon as an evil tyrant, I see him otherwise. He was a superior Frenchman, a man of action and bravado, who conquered much of Europe and had instated some fine precedents. He initiated critical road and sewer projects and established the Banque de France, our first central bank, one that we De Villes have long parlayed with to amass even greater wealth," he boasted with an odious air that was already choking Armand, as he went on, "Napoleon was the true heart and soul of France, affording the De Ville Financial Empire to flourish. And like the emperor, we decimated and conquered our rivals in a similar fashion." As Armand's repulsion accrued, like De Ville's devastating interest rates, Claude added, "And as *you* certainly must know, Mr. Arnolfini, Napoleon even had an affinity for fine art, not only for Jacques Louis David, but for many great masters."

Armand had enough and just snickered. "Yes, *Monsieur* De Ville, Napoleon had an affinity for art, all right, because he looted it." As Claude's face turned sour, Armand continued, "And Napoleon's reverence for art is questionable." Armand lifted up the statue, gazed deep into Napoleon's cold bronze eyes, then back at Claude's avaricious ones. "When your emperor conquered Venice, he snatched Veronese's colossal painting, *The Wedding at Cana*, and had it transferred to the Louvre, where he established his headquarters. Then, during preparations to marry his second wife, Marie Louise, he realized it simply didn't suit his wedding décor. So he ordered it to be destroyed." As Claude and even Andrea nearly gasped, Armand placed the statue back down and added, "Fortunately, Napoleon's minions disobeyed him. That's why the great painting survived and still hangs in the Louvre. A masterwork that should be in Venice."

Sergio stepped boldly toward his son, and whispered, "Armand! Is it truly necessary to demonstrate your knowledge of history?" Nervously, he looked at Claude, not wanting to lose this singular opportunity to locate a monumental work by Leonardo, and said, "Don't mind my son, *Monsieur* De Ville, I'm sure he meant no disrespect to the great name of Napoleon."

Claude glanced at Sergio, then back at Armand. He squinted, intensely. "Of course he didn't. As I've said, Napoleon was France's greatest leader."

Armand smiled. "Of course he was, because Napoleon was Italian. As was the sculptor of your precious statue—Antonio Canova."

As Sergio cringed, Claude's face turned indignant. He was about to fire back a retort, but realized he had no ammunition. He laughed. "*Touché! Signore* Arnolfini. Indeed, they both were." He glanced at Sergio. "Your son has great intellect *and* a fiery wit." He looked back at Armand. "That is why I wish to hire you, Armand. May I call you Armand?"

Armand chuckled. "You already did. *Twice.*"

With a round of laughter, which somewhat broke the ice and steadied Sergio's erratic heartbeat, Claude pointed to his plush, pleated sofa, a Riesener original. "Please, have a seat." He looked at Andrea. "And may I offer you something to drink?"

Andrea shook her head politely. "No, thank you. I'm sure my husband is eager to hear the details of this case."

"Ah, yes, I hear you are newlyweds. Congratulations."

As Andrea nodded her thanks, Claude retook his seat behind his elaborate desk and turned toward Armand. "Well, let's get right down to it. You see, I had the great fortune of living with Leonardo's masterpiece for many years as a child." He reached over and opened his cobalt blue and 18 karat gold Fabergé egg, and pulled out a cigarette. He waved it. "Any takers?"

As they each refused, he lit up the cigarette and closed the egg. Meanwhile, Armand was keenly aware that Claude's claim didn't jive with recorded history, as he inquired, "What do you mean, *you lived with it?* Do you mean Leonardo's original painting, or one of the copies made by several of his protégés?"

Claude rolled his eyes. He took a drag and irritably blew smoke out his nostrils. "The original, *Armand*...by the master himself. Naturally."

Giovanni Antonio Bazzi   Cesare da Sesto

Armand squinted and leaned closer. "How so? The *Leda* has been lost ever since da Vinci's death in 1519, with only one person, Cassiano dal Pozzo, saying he saw it at the Château de Fontainebleau in 1625. Then it disappeared for good."

Claude smirked. "I can see the doubt etched all over your face, Armand, but I assure you, we owned the original *Leda*. And, yes, you are very well informed. Cassiano did see it at the Fontainebleau. That's because my ancestor, Camille De Ville, had briefly put it on loan there. Soon after, it returned safely to our estate. But that's getting ahead of the initial acquisition, which took place seventy-eight years prior." He spun around in his swivel chair and pointed to the first of six portraits on the wall. "That is my great, great..." He rolled his eyes once again. "Oh, I forget how many *greats* precede his name, but suffice it to say, *that* is my illustrious ancestor, Jacque De Ville."

He spun around and looked back into Armand's eyes. "Jacque was the treasurer and dear friend of King Francis I, who reigned from 1515 until 1547." Taking another puff of his cigarette, Claude blew a stream of smoke out of the corner of his mouth and continued, "As *you* certainly must know, Armand, Leonardo was the king's personal artist, engineer, architect, and all around man of genius, who was graced with his own residency at Clos Lucé, which was connected to the king's palace by an underground passage."

Armand glanced at his father and Andrea, then intently back at Claude. The De Ville family's lineage was starting to paint a very clear and solid picture of provenance, Armand's chief concern, as Claude continued, "So, when King Francis died, he bequeathed to Jacque Leonardo's coveted painting of *Leda and the Swan*, along with a substantial sum of money, which enabled Jacque to start his own banking institution, which..." Claude pointed to all the walls around them, "you now see before you. The De Ville financial empire was Jacque's legacy."

Armand was more than intrigued—he was riveted, but also curious. "So, your family kept Leonardo's masterwork in your own private possession for hundreds of years, except for that one brief showing at the Fontainebleau, and never told a soul?"

Claude nodded. *"Oui, Monsieur.* It was the De Ville family's rightful possession. Why tell the world; that would have only enticed thieves." Claude took another deep drag, then haughtily turned up his nose and exhaled. He looked back down at the peasants before him, who could never comprehend the privileges of the mega-rich, and continued, this time drifting off into an ethereal mist of his fond memories: "As a child, my father, Pepé, would bring me down into the cellar of our estate to view the masterpiece every Sunday. It became a religious ritual, one that quickly eliminated the mindless monotony of sitting through church. It was liberating and inspiring. I grew very fond of it. Leonardo's mastery of anatomy, composition, and the ability to capture the inner thoughts and subtle movements of his subjects was unrivalled." He paused briefly, as the great work materialized in his mind's eye. Entranced, he went on, "And what a beauty to behold. Da Vinci's *Leda* was otherworldly, stunning, like Venus. Utter perfection. It was intoxicating."

Just then, Claude's gilded King Louis IV wall clock chimed, waking Claude out of his reverie. His eyes veered back toward Armand, only to notice Armand's dour expression. Claude's lips furled, as he said defensively, "You may think I was selfish, Armand, but you're wrong! Leonardo's painting was created not for a church or a museum, but for a patron's private enjoyment. You know that. And it was given to my ancestor with great affection by the king. *Leda and the Swan* was the De Ville family's prized heirloom." Firmly, he added, "It's mine! And *I want it back.*"

Armand stifled a retort, he was getting tired of hearing it was *Claude's* painting or the De Ville's private heirloom, and instead stuck to the business at hand. "Well, then tell me; how did it disappear?"

Claude leaned back in his chair and extinguished his cigarette in a lavish Hermès ashtray. His shoulders slumped. He looked into Sergio's eyes, then Andrea's, then back at Armand. His voice turned sullen. "It was at the onset of World War Two." He paused in thought, then continued, "You see, when Hitler invaded France, my father panicked. He was well aware of how the Nazis looted great works of art, so he called upon his friend, Ettore Bugatti, the famous

French automaker, to use his subterranean vault at his factory to store the work."

Armand rubbed his chin with growing interest, but needed to clear the air about misconstrued facts, not to mention giving Claude another dig, as he replied, "Well, another minor correction, Claude. Bugatti was also Italian." As Claude irritably bit his lips, Armand went on, "But what happened to the painting?" Eager to get to the punch line, he bulleted Claude: "Was it stolen by someone at the factory? By the Nazis? Or destroyed by an air raid? What?"

Claude just shrugged and flipped open his Fabergé egg once again. He slipped out another cigarette and lit up. After taking a deep drag, he exhaled. As he spoke, his words traveled upon a wave of smoke toward his guests' faces. "I don't know! *You're* the expert," he said snippily.

He opened the top drawer of his desk, pulled out his checkbook, and grasped his gold and diamond studded pen. He started filling out a check and, without looking up, said, "I'm issuing you a retainer of five thousand US dollars, Armand, to find my precious *Leda and the Swan* and return it to me. The balance shall be either twenty thousand dollars, if you fail, or one hundred thousand dollars, if you succeed." Having finished filling out the check, he lifted it up and looked at Armand. "Is that agreeable?"

As Andrea and Sergio smiled, relieved to have finally reached this historic moment, Armand simply chuckled.

Sergio and Andrea's heads snapped in his direction, as Armand glanced around Claude's lavish office, and said, "Claude, I see you're a man who knows the value of things. And not only am *I* worth more than that, but as you surely know, Leonardo's lost *Leda* is worth a helluva lot more than a hundred and five thousand dollars. In fact, *Leda and the Swan* is so coveted, that some predict that, if found, it would rival the most famous painting in the world; namely da Vinci's own *Mona Lisa*. So, this is a very special case and requires a unique payment plan. And your little finder's fee is not a reasonable percentage of the *Leda*'s total market value."

Claude's face cracked with a devious smile. He ripped up the check. "You're even smarter and more savvy than the legendary reputation that precedes you, Mr. Arnolfini. I apologize if I insulted you. However, while I agree that the *Leda* is worth far more than my offer, I question your expertise regarding it rivaling the *Mona Lisa*. Not that I wouldn't want my *Leda* to do so, but I'm curious to know how you can justify that?"

Armand unbuttoned his jacket and leaned back comfortably and confidently into De Ville's vintage sofa. "Simple, Claude, because *Leda and the Swan* was the only painting by Leonardo of a pagan myth. I'm sure you were aware of that during your Sunday rituals while avoiding church." As Claude squinted and crossed his arms, Armand went on, "Meanwhile, Leonardo's entire oeuvre consisted of works glorifying the Christian religion, private portraits, or even secular in nature, such as the *Battle of Anghiari*, or the Sforzas' equestrian monument. However, *Leda* was unique, and in more ways than one." Flashing through Armand's mind were the sketches Leonardo left behind of Leda's

complex network of braided hair, giving a hint at what the masterpiece might have looked like, as he launched into a concise explanation of the Leda tale, of which all ears paid heed.

Armand explained how the story of *Leda and the Swan* emanated from the often-bizarre realms of Greek mythology. Full of exotic and erotic overtones, it told how Zeus transformed himself into a swan to fool and seduce the mortal princess Leda. That was to fulfill his odd penchant for fornicating with humans, whereby creating demigods in his lustful wake. To some, however, it also symbolized the folly of women to be easily deceived.

While most artists portrayed this scene in graphic, erotic detail, often with obscene positions of bestial sex, Leonardo—in his atypical and profound manner—had created a tender-loving vision of Leda, one that evaded the carnal act and focused on the beauty of motherhood and procreation. Standing naked with the swan god by her side, Leonardo's *Leda* gazed lovingly at two cracked eggshells on the ground, each of which had given birth to a set of twins that she and Zeus bequeathed to the world, namely Helen (who would become Helen of Troy) and Clytemnestra, along with Castor and Pollux. Hence, Leonardo turned what others portrayed as lust and depravity into a divine vision of love and fertility.

As Armand finished his mini lecture, Andrea smiled with admiration, while De Ville sat pensive, almost in a trance. Meanwhile, Sergio's eyes veered back and forth, between his bold and brilliant son and at De Ville, hoping they would come to a resolution and seal the deal. The thought of losing this opportunity weighed more on Sergio's mind than the mere weight of gold bullion in dollars, as the colossal weight of perhaps Western civilization's most priceless masterpiece was, to Sergio, equal to the weight of the Earth itself. Feeling as if Atlas, Sergio found it hard to manage the pressure bearing down on him, and finally spoke, "Well, gentlemen? What will it be?"

De Ville awoke from his foray and glanced at Sergio, then over at Armand. "Uh, yes, very well put," he said as he now realized that the *Leda* was far more valuable than even he had imagined. He smiled. "So, here's my revised offer: A twenty-five thousand dollar retainer, twenty-five thousand more if you fail, and a five percent commission of the current market value of the painting, *if* you return it to me in good condition."

Once again Armand chuckled.

Andrea twitched nervously, while Sergio leapt frantically back into the conversation. "Armand! For God's sake, settle up with him and let's get this show on the road."

Armand calmly looked at his father and raised his index finger. "*Un minuto.*" He gazed back at De Ville. "Claude, you just added 'in good condition.' I can make no guarantees as to the condition I'll find it in. Furthermore, five percent is unacceptable. Make it ten percent, and returned in *as is* condition, and we have a deal."

De Ville's lips twisted as his eyes gazed irritably down at his desktop, focusing on the numbers flashing in his calculating mind. He was accustomed to dictating his terms, not negotiating them, especially with a man who had the temerity to needle *him*—a De Ville, a proud and eminent Frenchman—with his porcupine-like tongue. After a brief moment, of which Sergio and Andrea held their breaths, De Ville looked up and said, "That's an awful lot of money to find my lost *Leda*, Mr. Arnolfini. I'm sure I could hire another private investigator at a much cheaper rate."

"You most certainly can," Armand said as he sat upright and glanced around Claude's posh office. "But, by the looks of things, it's clear that you know the old adage; you get what you pay for. I don't see any $10.99 posters hanging on your walls, nor is your furniture laminated-pressboard by IKEA. Each piece is a vintage work of art by master craftsmen, made out of the finest materials." Armand glanced down at Claude's desk. "Such as that beautiful desk, which appears to be by André Boulle. I love the combination of ebony and tortoiseshell marquetry with gilded accents. It's quite exquisite. And dear me, even your ashtray is not some two-dollar trinket from Sears; it's at least an $800 Hermès special, with 18 karat gold trim. You know quality when you see it, Claude, and *I'm* sitting right here. Open your eyes." As Claude couldn't help but smile, enjoying Arnolfini's impressive presentation, Armand continued, "And let me say this: *if* the *Leda* truly exists, I *will* find it. There are very few private eyes in this line of work. It's an extremely specialized field. So, if you want to piss away your money on some penny-ante P.I., who will drag out this investigation for months or even years, and nickel and dime you with mounting miscellaneous fees—something I'm sure *you're* an expert at—then be my guest."

As Andrea nervously looked on and Sergio clutched his heart, Claude cracked a mysterious smile, which soon withered, as he just sat pensive and mute. Only the ticking of the King Louis IV wall clock could be heard as the seconds passed. Sergio began to sweat and took deep noticeable breaths, as if a Lamaze exercise, while Claude indecisively shook his head, then gazed at his statue of Napoleon.

Armand noticed. "*He* never would have procrastinated, Claude. Napoleon knew when to strike, he was successful because of his quicksilver decisions." As Claude gazed up, startled, Armand added, "So, what's it going to be?" He glanced at his watch. "I have a honeymoon I could be enjoying."

Claude glanced at Andrea, who smiled, then back at Armand. He paused briefly, then uttered, "Very well. But the current market value of my *Leda* will be assessed by a third party, someone we both must agree upon."

Armand stood up. "Fair enough. We have a deal."

As Sergio and Andrea sighed, Claude dutifully reached into his drawer. "Give me a minute, I'll draw up the contract."

"That won't be necessary," Armand said firmly. "We can do that later. It's crucial that I jump on this case immediately."

Claude squinted, while Sergio leapt to his feet and patted Armand on the back. "Good boy!" With a beaming grin, he walked over and shook Claude's hand vigorously. "Thank God you two ironed this out! You won't regret it, *Monsieur* De Ville."

De Ville stood up. "I hope not." He handed Armand the check. "As I've stated, there's no way of knowing if the painting even survived the war. But if it did, I *must* have it. I'm counting on you."

"Understood," Armand said, as he handed Andrea the check.

Andrea flinched with surprise. "Why are you giving it to me?"

"We're married now, and some time ago I said that you'd make an excellent treasurer. So, the job is yours."

"Okay, fine, dear," Andrea said, as she leaned toward his ear and whispered jokingly, "But we never talked about my salary."

Armand chuckled, and whispered back, "We'll discuss that later. After all, there *are* other forms of payment." He winked, then turned back toward De Ville. "Is there anything else you can tell me?"

Claude nodded and walked toward his exquisite Riesener bookcase, stocked with first editions, precious artifacts, and in one cubical, a scaled model of the 1932 Bugatti Royale, Coupe De Ville Binder. He lifted up the classic car and looked at Armand. "Ettore Bugatti only built seven of these beauties, this one being the second one, and aptly named Coupe *De Ville*." He placed it gently back down and added, "Naturally, that was in homage to my father."

Armand gazed at the beautifully designed classic with intensity. "I'm a bit of a car enthusiast myself. I own several old classics, but nothing like this. The Bugatti Royale has always been one of my favorites." His eyes drifted up to Claude's icy blue irises. "If your father was close friends with Ettore, I imagine you must have stayed in contact with the Bugatti family, yes?"

Claude's expression soured. "Actually, no. There was a big falling out during the war years." Claude walked back to his desk, lit up another cigarette, and sat down. A wave of melancholy washed over him once again as he gazed solemnly into space, then back up at Armand.

Claude explained how Bugatti had developed the luxurious car exclusively for royalty. Unfortunately, the timing was impeccably wrong. The Great Depression hit and severely damaged the Bugatti Company. Meanwhile, Ettore's son Jean died while test-driving one of his cars in 1939. With the advent of the war, the Nazis began commandeering businesses, and Ettore was forced to sell his company to the Germans at below market value. Claude added, "Bugatti was devastated. With his life spiraling into a black hole, Ettore became bitter, my father being just one casualty."

Claude's hand shook as he took another drag. As he exhaled, an air of animus reshaped his words. "So, between their relationship falling apart and the damn Nazis gaining control of the factory, my father lost the ability to gain access to the factory's underground vault. We suspect that the Nazi pigs never located the hidden vault, but that's mere conjecture."

Claude irritably extinguished his cigarette in his dazzling ashtray and forcefully stood up. "So, I have no damn clue what happened to my precious *Leda*. And I strongly advise you to avoid contacting any surviving Bugattis, Armand, because it would yield nothing of value. They won't even return my phone calls, the dirty bastards!"

He grasped Armand's shoulder and edged him toward the door. "I apologize for getting so emotional, but Ettore and that family did much to kill my father. Not overtly, but psychologically and financially. I won't go into details, but suffice it to say, there's no love between our families."

Sergio and Andrea uncomfortably glanced at each other, then followed them toward the door, as Armand asked several questions, which Claude answered tersely. He then added, "The Bugatti factory is located in Molsheim, right here in France. It was largely destroyed during the war and remains in ruins, but that would be the place *I* would start my investigation." Abruptly, he edged Armand out of his office, as Sergio and Andrea squeezed by him and also stepped into the main lobby. Claude closed the door halfway, his face peering out. "My secretary can help you with anything else you need. Keep me posted. Good luck!" With that, Claude firmly closed the door.

The trio looked at one another and shrugged as they marched toward the exit. Meanwhile, Andrea paused at the secretary's desk and asked, "Is he always that odd?"

The secretary glanced cautiously at De Ville's door, then back at Andrea. "He's a billionaire," she whispered. "They're *all* odd. If they were normal there wouldn't be any billionaires."

Twenty minutes later, Armand rented a new 1985 Renault Fuego, and the trio sped from Paris toward Molsheim, in the Alsace region of France. Andrea sat in the passenger's seat, enjoying her role as navigator, while Sergio took a nap in the back seat. On the radio, Tears for Fears new hit, *Everybody Wants to Rule the World*, played, as visions of Claude De Ville and Napoleon flashed through Armand's mind.

Four and half hours later, they arrived in the town of Molsheim, a mere twenty kilometers away from the West German border. Sergio crawled out of the back seat and stood up to stretch his aching, old back, while Andrea ran into the *Quatre Saisons Café* to relieve herself.

Armand peered around at the quaint village. Against Claude's advice, he had contacted Giacomo Bugatti, Ettore's grandson, upon leaving Paris and setup an appointment to meet him at the Bugatti mansion. Armand glanced at his watch. He still had an hour to kill, and decided they should grab a bite to eat at the café.

As the threesome ate lunch, Andrea skimmed through a *Fodor's* travel guide. She smiled. "Look at this, we can stay at Hotel Le Bugatti."

Sergio swallowed a slice of his raspberry crepe and chuckled. "How appropriate. Money talks."

"Yes," Armand said. "And let's just hope Giacomo Bugatti talks, *a lot* about where the lost *Leda* might be."

Andrea's eyes widened with surprise. "Bugatti!? De Ville said we shouldn't contact them?"

"Exactly, that's why I did."

Sergio chuckled with appreciation, while Andrea paused, then also giggled as she poured sugar in her coffee and began to stir. Then she stopped. "But do you really think a Bugatti will have anything of value to tell us?"

Armand shrugged. "It's hard to tell, but he must know something about it, even if it's the worst news imaginable, that the Nazis stole it or destroyed it in a bombing raid."

Sergio gasped. "Don't even think along those lines, Armand. I have to believe it survives, somewhere. Leonardo left us so few finished paintings, and, as you know, this was cited as one that the master actually completed. So, it would be sinful if it was...well...I dare not even think of it."

"Pop, you know life is not kind, nor are people intelligent. Look at how those morons at the refectory of Santa Maria delle Grazie cut a doorway into the bottom of da Vinci's fresco of the *Last Supper*, lopping off Jesus' feet, or how some other fool cut the head of Leonardo's *Saint Jerome* out of the wood panel to make a stool. Fortunately Jerome's severed head was found, reattached, and repaired, but there's no end to how stupid people can be with priceless works of art."

Andrea's face twisted with astonishment. "Someone actually cut Saint Jerome's head out to make *a stool*?"

Sergio intervened, "Yes, my dear. It's true. Actually the walnut panel it was painted on was cut up into *five* separate pieces. God knows what for. But *Saint Jerome* happens to be another one of Leonardo's unfinished masterworks." He wiped the raspberry compote off his lips. "It's only a painterly sketch in amber undertones and accented with highlights. But what highlights they are!" His old but handsome face illuminated with admiration as he expounded upon it further. "Leonardo knew how to give life to an inert piece of wood. The intensity of Jerome's expression, his flawless anatomy, and the overall composition give all indications that—if Leonardo had

finished it—it, too, would sit at the apex of Renaissance art." He paused briefly, and added with reverence, "No artist in his day, or before him, ever achieved the excellence that his unerring eye and hand did when fully committed."

Andrea ingested Sergio's moving words, then looked at Armand. "But when we were in Ghent, you praised Jan van Eyck as the greatest technician of his day."

"Yes, he was," Armand said as he swallowed a morsel of quiche Lorraine. "Van Eyck's rendering of inanimate objects *was* impeccable, and his use of perspective *was* revolutionary. However, his figures often looked like cadavers or plastic dolls, as did those of most artists at that time. The study of anatomy was just beginning to be reborn after a millennium of censure from the Church, so only a handful of artists were taught anatomy. And certainly, no artist performed autopsies like Leonardo, who personally dissected over thirty bodies and made significant scientific contributions. Some of his discoveries debunked the long-held and erroneous beliefs of Galen and the ancient Greeks, while others were only discovered several centuries later, since his treatise on anatomy was unfortunately never published." As Andrea listened with awe, Armand went on, "So, you see, very few of Leonardo's peers devoted much time and analysis as to how the tiniest of muscles and sinews react when motivated by human emotions." Stirring his cappuccino, he added, "Basically, Leonardo combined the keen observation of an artist with the anatomical precision of a scientist. And that knowledge allowed his talented hands to transform static oil and paint into glowing renditions of animated life."

As the *garcon* issued Armand the check, Sergio grabbed his jacket, eager to begin their investigation, while Andrea became more intrigued by the Renaissance master as she grasped her purse.

The trio exited the café and hopped back into the Renault. Armand drove six kilometers through the countrified streets toward the Bugatti estate, taking in the scenic splendor of France. As they approached the imposing mansion, the crackling sound of gravel under their tires broke the silence of the still air.

Standing on the front terrace was Giacomo Bugatti—grandson to the famous founder and inventor, Ettore—who walked down to greet them. Giacomo was in his early thirties, five-feet-eight with slick black hair and dressed immaculately in a Dormeuil pinstripe suit.

After a brief round of introductions, Giacomo said, "So, you say you're in search of the lost *Leda*. How could *I* possibly help?"

Armand hesitated, then said, "Well, I'll pull no punches. Claude De Ville mentioned you might know something regarding its whereabouts."

Giacomo's amicable smile vanished. *"Claude De Ville! Ha!"* He rolled his eyes. "So, that conniving vulture put you up to this, huh? I should have known."

Sergio raised his hand. "Hold on, son! Claude said he tried calling you."

Giacomo glanced at Sergio. "No he didn't. *Never.* He wouldn't have the nerve."

"We're not in this to satisfy Claude," Armand interjected. "Despite him giving me a retainer to start this investigation, the magnitude of Leonardo's lost work exceeds Claude's selfish desires. That's why I also declined signing a contract with him. If the *Leda* is found, it will end up on the wall of a public museum, not incarcerated in De Ville's private dungeon."

Andrea looked on, astonished, while Sergio's heart swelled with admiration.

Meanwhile, Armand continued, "Once the art world finds out about this startling discovery—*if*, and that's a big *if*, it surfaces—there will be many wealthy philanthropists and museums clamoring for it, whom I have connections with. So I, in all good conscience, could never deprive the world of this painting's glory by handing it over to an egotistical, selfish snob like Claude De Ville for his personal pleasure."

Giacomo studied Armand's face. "Although that's very altruistic, Mr. Arnolfini, that doesn't give me much confidence that I'm speaking with someone who is trustworthy. If you betrayed your employer, how could *I* possibly trust you?"

"Because it didn't take long for me to discern De Ville's greedy disposition during our meeting." With a tinge of revulsion in his voice, he continued, "And he's *a liar*. Just before he rudely shoved us out of his office, I had asked him if he had documentation of King Francis bequeathing the painting to Jacque, his ancestor. He had none. Furthermore, he refused to speak about the details of your feud. And knowing that you loathe him as much as he does you, I can trust *you* that *our* secret will be kept confidential."

Giacomo grinned. "Well, that makes me feel a whole lot better." His tense shoulders relaxed. "Yes, not only does Claude have no tangible evidence of King Francis' will, but, for what it's worth, his father Pepe had even boasted to my grandfather how Jacque De Ville stole the painting upon the king's death, along with embezzling millions of francs to start his financial empire. You can also take that as hearsay, but I'll swear on my grandfather's grave that it's the unvarnished truth." Giacomo's face crumpled, looking like he ate a rotten egg, as he added, "In a nutshell, the De Ville family is a lying pack of parasites. They're elitist gangsters who have fleeced millions for well over five centuries. And Claude is just the latest incarnation of evil."

Armand nodded thoughtfully, then capriciously smiled. "I wonder; by any chance, is Claude's mother Cruella?"

As Andrea laughed, Giacomo squinted, not privy to the Disney cartoon, as he replied, "No, I don't think so. Why?"

Now Armand laughed. "Never mind. But we would like to know what happened to your factory during the war years, and the vault?"

"Unfortunately, the Molsheim factory was destroyed," Giacomo said. "To my knowledge, so, too, was the vault during the blitzkrieg. At least that's what the surveyors who inspected the site after the war had told us." He paused, then said, "However, after the Nazis forced my grandfather to hand over the company, his lead engineer, Henri DuPont, and several laborers remained in the Germans' employ. Perhaps they might know something."

Sergio interjected excitedly, "Is Henri DuPont still alive?"

Giacomo turned toward Sergio. "Yes, he's an old bugger, in his eighties, but he still has his marbles."

Sergio's feathers were ruffled. "Listen young fella, as you can see, I'm no kid myself, and I still have *my* marbles!"

As they all chuckled, Armand said, "Yes, we'd appreciate the opportunity to speak with Henri, if that's at all possible?"

Giacomo nodded. "Why certainly. But if Henri knew where the painting was, I'm sure he would have mentioned it years ago, either to my grandfather or someone else in my family."

"That's not always the case," Armand replied. "There are many variables that come into play in situations like this. Whether it's hush money, fear, or even apathy, there are numerous reasons why people do what they do. Or he may legitimately know nothing...or perhaps who took it, or God forbid, who destroyed it. So, I'm curious to hear Henri's perspective, especially being that he was an eyewitness."

"Consider it done," Giacomo said. "I'll have my butler call him. In the meantime, allow me to show you around."

Giacomo summoned and instructed his butler, then escorted the Arnolfinis through the main rooms of the mansion, from its grand dining hall and posh living room to his grandfather's den, replete with models of his classic cars and even one of the revolutionary Model 100 racing plane. The futuristic aircraft had been built specifically for an air show in 1939 but missed the deadline. When Nazi troops invaded France, Ettore dismantled the plane and hid the parts and plans in his factory's vault to avoid falling into the hands of the enemy. After the war, it was never built to completion, since the plans were presumed destroyed and Ettore died in 1947.

Armand was intrigued. "So, your grandfather stored his precious plane in his vault along with da Vinci's priceless painting?"

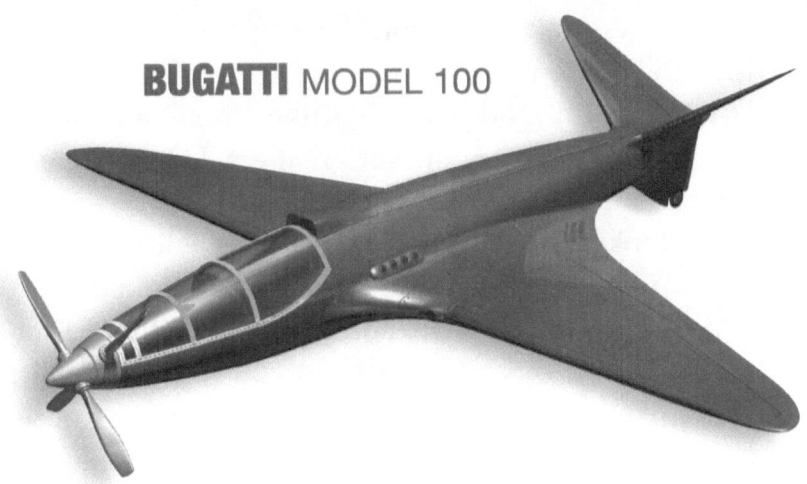

BUGATTI MODEL 100

Giacomo nodded. "Yes. That was the big secret, all right. But, the site was so badly damaged, no one, even the surveyors, thought anything could have survived. Everything was literally pulverized. I suspect my grandfather must have shuttered at the mere thought of viewing the masterpiece being damaged beyond recognition."

Just then, they heard a car pull up the gravel driveway. Sergio eagerly peered out the window. "It's a taxi! He's here!"

The entourage scurried outside and was greeted by Henri DuPont. Henri was five feet five, wore round glasses, a beige beret, and hobbled toward them with his cane. In his thick French accent he said, *"Salutations à tous."* His eyes finally connected with Sergio's. "Ah! Especially *you!*" he exclaimed with a grin. "Sergio. Yes, Sergio Arnolfini! That's your name. We met some forty years ago at the Uffizi Gallery, when you were its eminent curator. I never forget a face or a name."

Sergio was delighted to be remembered, but ashamed *he* couldn't remember Henri, especially in front of Giacomo, whom he recently scolded for not losing his marbles. Feigning a smile of recognition, he responded, "Ah, *si, si.* The Uffizi, the golden days of my life."

Armand could read his father like a book and stepped in to save face. "And speaking of great art, Henri, we are in search of da Vinci's lost *Leda and the Swan.*"

Henri looked at Armand as his eyes widened, while Armand continued, "Giacomo says you worked in the Bugatti factory where De Ville and Ettore had stored it in an underground vault. By any chance, do you recall seeing it?"

Henri fixed the glasses on his large aquiline nose to focus his blurry gaze. "Well, *Monsieur*, my eyes may have failed me in old age, but I assure you, they were sharp as a rapier during the war."

As everyone's attention was now glued to the little old man's words, Henri continued, "I had the remarkable good fortune of seeing Leonardo's masterpiece. It was only once, when Ettore secretly escorted me down into the vault. He entrusted its secrecy to but only a very select few, of which I take great pride in being one so lucky. But that was well before he was forced to hand over his factory to those Nazi thugs."

Armand stepped closer to DuPont, his curiosity piqued. To be speaking with someone who actually laid eyes on a missing masterpiece was always a thrill for Armand, and he now pressed Henri for more details. "When the Nazis took over, what happened then? Did they know the painting was stored in the vault?"

Henri shook his head adamantly. "No, *Monsieur*. They had no idea whatsoever. We in the resistance made sure of that. As double insurance, Ettore had even paid all of us who remained in the Nazis' employ not to speak about it, or even to mention that a hidden vault existed."

Sergio interjected, "Well, thank God for that."

Meanwhile, Andrea was equally riveted, and asked, "But what happened after that?"

Henri's head jerked from one inquisitor to the next, becoming somewhat disoriented as he grasped his cane to steady himself. Armand clutched his arm and noticed a bench near the mansion's entrance. "Can I help you to a seat, *Monsieur* DuPont?"

Relieved by Armand's assistance, Henri nodded and was escorted to the bench. The entourage crowded around him while Giacomo summoned his butler to bring them all refreshments.

As birds chirped and the wind rustled the nearby trees and manicured gardens, the butler returned with drinks and a tray of *hors d'oeuvres*.

After a brief respite, Armand resumed the inquiry. "If the Germans never knew about the vault, what happened to the painting?"

Henri swallowed a piece of Roquefort cheese with a sip of wine, then looked up at Armand. "I wish I knew. It was a tumultuous time. The evil eyes of our Nazi superiors were constantly upon us, including those of the Gestapo. Fear ruled and ruined many lives, *Monsieur*. It's hard to create in words what we lived through. But I always suspected Alfonse Moreau. I just never trusted that man."

Armand sat beside Henri. "Who was Alfonse Moreau? And why didn't you trust him?"

Henri shifted sideways to get a better view of Armand. "Alfonse was our janitor. A lowly and mentally feeble fella, who had been caught several times stealing auto parts by sticking them in trash cans and coming back later in the night to retrieve them."

Andrea interjected, "But stealing auto parts is not the same as stealing a large and valuable painting, *Monsieur* DuPont." Henri's head swiveled toward the sound of her voice. "Yes, you are quite right, *Madame*. But I had seen Alfonse several times snooping around the secret entrance to the vault. And knowing of his unethical disposition, I simply never trusted him. I was raised to excel at whatever I engaged my mind in, and that's why I studied hard and earned my way into École Polytechnique to study engineering. Meanwhile, Alphonse was a man who expected rewards without effort. As far as I know, he dropped out of school, never opened a book, never desired to learn new things, and simply never cared to work to *earn* a better living for himself or his poor family, whom I believe abandoned him."

"Well, that gives motive, *Monsieur* DuPont," Armand said. "But no clear evidence. However, that's a good place to start, that is, *after* I excavate the old factory to uncover the vault."

Everyone turned and looked at Armand, as Giacomo said, "Armand, as I told you, the factory was devastated. It's under mounds of rubble, which certainly must have crushed the underground vault, like the surveyors said."

"Well, I can't take it upon idle observation that it was destroyed or that the *Leda* is not down there. I need to see it with my own eyes. To paraphrase Leonardo, who refused to accept the hypotheses of the old Greek philosophers, one must always turn to nature to learn the truth. And by doing so he proved many of them wrong."

Over the next two days, excavators rolled over the old Bugatti factory, digging up the rubble that buried the past and, as the three Arnolfinis hoped, perhaps a priceless work of art. Mounds of debris were piled up on the outskirts of the site as the machines cleared away the area where Henri had indicated the vault was located. As the clawed arm of one backhoe dug down some fifteen feet through the rubble it suddenly struck a piece of metal!

"That's it!" Sergio bellowed, as Armand and Andrea's eyes zeroed in on the spot.

The steel door was badly mangled and rusted shut.

Armand looked at Andrea then his father. "That's a great sign. If the door is still somewhat intact, that means it protected whatever is inside the vault." He looked at the backhoe operator. "Go ahead, rip it open!"

With that, the claw of the machine reached down and tore the rusted steel door off its hinges.

Armand and crew wasted no time as they darted inside, wielding flashlights. The chamber was approximately twenty feet square and largely vacant. As their beams of light illuminated the concrete walls and mostly barren shelves, their hearts dropped. Not even the Model 100 aircraft parts or plans were to be found. Sergio nearly cried as a wave of nausea came over him. He had placed so much faith that the lost *Leda* would still be sitting in its place, untouched and in sound condition, that the shock was too much for his aging body. He staggered.

Andrea noticed and immediately dropped her flashlight to grab his arms and steady him. "Are you all right, Dad?" she asked worriedly.

Armand swiveled around. "Pop! What is it?"

Sergio closed his eyes and took deep breaths, then finally uttered, "I'll be all right...I...think." His torso wavered and his knees buckled.

Armand dashed over and helped Andrea support him. They walked him out into the fresh air and sat him down on a large chunk of debris. One of the construction workers rushed over with a bottle of water. Sergio sipped, but seconds later vomited.

"You need to rest, Papa," Armand said. "That's it. I'm arranging a flight to get you home. And I'm calling Paolo to keep an eye on you."

Sergio looked up at Armand. "You're *not* my father, *son*." Sounding painfully like a child, he protested, "I don't want to go home! And I don't need my blind old buddy to babysit me." He glanced back at the vault. "We hit a dead end, Armand. But there has to be another lead. There just has to be."

"There is, Pop. Remember, Henri mentioned Alphonse Moreau?"

Sergio squinted, then he once again feigned remembering. "Uh, yes, yes, *of course* I remember." He gazed piercingly up at Armand. "Don't patronize me, Armand!"

Armand knew that his father was entering the early stages of dementia or possibly Alzheimer's and it killed him to have to step in like a father figure. Sitting before him was the brilliant man who graduated magna cum laude, curated the world-renowned Uffizi Gallery, was a distinguished professor of art history at the Florence Academy, and more importantly, shaped Armand's life, who was now starting to lose the precious mental facilities that had nurtured and influenced Armand and countless students.

Armand fought back the tears that threatened to breach his eyes and swallowed hard. "Pop, I'm not patronizing you. You're the smartest man I know, one I've always admired and aspired to emulate. But this case is taking its toll on you, emotionally and now physically." He grabbed both of his father's hands and looked deep into his eyes. "I know how important Leonardo and his legacy is to you. And I swear to do everything in my power to find the lost *Leda*, if it exists, and return it, not to De Ville, but to the world."

Sergio managed to smile. "Yes, my son, you made me happy beyond words to outwit and foil De Ville's selfish plans. The thought of that wretch commandeering this masterpiece once again, never to see the light of day, would be a travesty."

"You taught me to always do the right thing, Pop, regardless of whether or not it's at a financial gain or loss." Armand paused in brief reflection as a mysterious *Mona Lisaesque* smile came across his face. "But it certainly would've felt nice to get a ten percent commission on the *Leda*, Pop, because I can just imagine the hundreds of millions it will fetch, *if* I find it."

Sergio looked at his son with deep admiration and nodded with a warm smile. "Yes, that's an enormous windfall to walk away from. Thankfully, I've taught you well. You've made a tough and very benevolent decision, one that not many would have done. Correction, *no one* would have done. You have no idea how crucial you are, having retrieved numerous masterworks from oblivion. But, more importantly, how special you are to *me*, Armand. You're beyond priceless; you're a divine gift. I'm so proud of you."

Armand swallowed hard, deeply touched. "Thank you, Pop. That sentiment alone is worth more than several hundred million dollars."

As Sergio's eyes welled with emotion, Armand immediately changed the subject, knowing that his father's loving tears would only trigger his own, as he said, "Okay, then it's settled. Home you go." As Sergio sequestered his tears and nodded, Armand continued, "Andrea and I will handle this. You need to take care of yourself, at least until I can get back to Florence and speak with your doctors. And don't be stubborn, let Paolo help you, you've known each other since childhood. I'll make the arrangements."

The next day Sergio caught a flight back to Florence, as Armand and Andrea saw him off. Afterwards, the newlyweds drove back to Hotel Le Bugatti. Eating lunch at the hotel's café, the couple sat in silence, Andrea buttering her toast and Armand just gazing at his frothy cup of cappuccino. The dejection of not finding *Leda and the Swan* in the vault had taken its toll on all parties involved, as Armand picked up this spoon and mechanically stirred the hot coffee.

Andrea finally looked at him. "It's nice that you told your father that we had another lead with Alfonse Moreau, Armand. But Henri and Giacomo had no idea where to find him. So, what now?"

Armand managed to break his manikin-like gaze and looked up into her magnetic eyes. "You really *are* beautiful."

Andrea recoiled. "Where did *that* come from?"

Armand smiled. "From the heart."

Andrea blushed. "Well, thank you, sweetheart. But did you even hear what I said?"

He finally picked up his cup and took a sip, then said, "Of course. But it was a question I have no answer for. So, the first thing I saw was *you*, and that *was* something I could respond to."

Andrea chuckled. "Okay, I do love your sense of logic, but we must do something."

"Naturally. We must, it's our honeymoon; the one you generously put aside to go on this wild *Swan* expedition." As Andrea giggled, Armand looked deep into her eyes with admiration. "I must say, the way you jumped into this case, with such vitality and enthusiasm, really surprised *and* energized me. You've made the job I've always enjoyed even more thrilling and priceless. I can't thank you enough for being my wife *and* investigative partner."

Andrea blushed. "You really *are* adorable, Armand. But I don't consider myself a partner, or even an investigator, for that matter. I have much to learn. And once we get back home, I do have my curator job at the P.T. Barnum Museum. So, my input *will* be limited. But for the record, I could never think of being married to anyone else but you." She reached over and tenderly grasped his hand. "You're an amazing man. I love you dearly." She looked adoringly into his eyes, then squeezed his hand tight. *"But,* what are we going to do *now*!?"

Armand laughed, breaking him out of his romantic stupor. "Okay!" he said with a chuckle. "I'll figure something out."

As he looked at her beautifully crafted face and into her alluring eyes, he couldn't help his romantic heart from taking the reins once again, as he said, "But for now, let's just enjoy our meal and this moment. After all, it's a prerequisite to a great relationship to share good food together and open one's heart. One never knows when the good Lord has other plans for us. I learned that the hard way with Cynthia. So I *will* cherish the moments we share together, because there's truly nothing else in this world more important to me than you. You've grown in my heart, not like a foreign substance, but like the tissue itself...intertwining and strengthening it with every beat."

Andrea's face blossomed with a serene smile. "Well, now you're melting *my* heart." She peered down at her wedding and engagement rings, then back up. "But, you're right. I suppose most people get caught up in life and don't take the time to reflect on what matters most." She glanced down at her grilled salmon, then lifted her glass of white Burgundy. "Let's toast to *us!*"

Armand shoved his customary cup of cappuccino aside and lifted his glass of wine. He clinked glasses with his *amore* and took a sip. After a delightful meal and engaging conversation, the newlyweds retreated to their hotel room for some extra curricular activity.

After showering and freshening up, the couple hopped in their rented Renault and took a drive. Instead of his typical itinerary, of exploring historic or cultural sites, Armand was simply in the mood to breathe in the countryside and experience the French way of life. Their mini tour included driving through charming villages and past rustic farms and stopping to speak with farmers, mechanics, shopkeepers, and, in essence, the unsung, beating heart of France. Five hours later, they returned to the town of Molsheim. As they passed an art bookstore, Andrea called out, "Stop! Let's check it out."

Armand cut the wheel and swiftly parked the car. "What's so pressing about *Maurice's Librairie d'art*?"

Andrea hopped out. "If I'm going to be your Watson, Sherlock, I need to study up."

Armand chuckled as he got out and followed her. As they walked toward the entrance she said, "I hate to admit this, but even though I'm a curator of a museum, I don't feel like I have much creativity in my genes." As she pushed open the door, she added, "You have an uncanny eye, but I can hardly recognize a great work of art when I see it."

"Oh stop!" Armand said, "You certainly can, just look in the mirror!"

Andrea looked back over her shoulder. "Your flattery will get you everywhere!"

"It already did, just a few hours ago," Armand said, as Andrea entered the store with a glowing smile.

Her eyes scanned the covers of various art books, while Armand followed behind, his eyes fixated more on his beautiful new bride than any art book.

The old shopkeeper at the counter queried, "*Que cherchez-vous?* (What are you looking for?)"

Andrea looked over and replied, "*Parlez vous Anglais?*"

"*Oui, Madame*, I mean yes, of course," he replied.

"I'm looking for books on Leonardo da Vinci."

"Ah, Leonardo," the man said as he adjusted his glasses. "*Oui*, we have several nicely illustrated books on the great master. Anything in particular? His paintings, engineering, architecture, anatomy, botany, flight…dear me, the list goes on!"

"Actually, yes," she said. "Do you have any books about his *Leda and the Swan*?"

The old man squinted. "That's rather peculiar."

"Why is that?"

The man hobbled his way out from behind the counter. "Because it's not something anyone has ever asked for in all my years in business, expect for the odd old fellow who came in here about two months ago."

Armand's eyes snapped open wide as he walked toward the old man. "What odd fellow? Do you remember his name?"

Meanwhile, Andrea briskly stepped up alongside Armand, also peering into the cute old man's eyes.

Somewhat startled, the elderly man took a step backward and looked up at them. "Are you Interpol? What did this man do?"

Armand smiled. "No, I'm a private investigator." He glanced at Andrea. "And *we're* looking for Leonardo's lost *Leda and the Swan*. Do you happen to know the man's name?"

As Armand showed the old man his credentials and they exchanged names, Maurice readjusted his glasses and rubbed his chin. "Yes, I believe it was Arnold Mor...no, no, it was Alfonse. Yes, that's it. Alfonse Moreau."

Armand and Andrea glanced at each other, as Armand said, "Alfonse Moreau? Are you sure?"

"Quite sure," Maurice said. "So, you think that odd fellow might be the culprit?"

"It's a slight possibility," Armand said. "And if not, perhaps he knows who might have taken it or if it was destroyed during the war."

"Well, *Monsieur*, fortune shines on you," Maurice said. "Because that fellow had also ordered two books, which I had delivered to him by post. Therefore, I have his address."

"That's fantastic!" Andrea blurted. "She turned toward Armand. "What a break. It's a good thing I made you stop here, aye, Sherlock?"

Armand chuckled. "Yes, Watson. I do say, bloody-well good, ol' chap." He turned toward Maurice, who giggled at their playful banter and smiled. Perceptively, he noticed the shiny new wedding bands on their fingers. "I reckon you two are newlyweds, yes?"

Armand and Andrea were taken aback. With Armand being forty and Andrea thirty-eight, they didn't quite view themselves as the typical young wedding couple, as Andrea said, "Yes, we are. How did you know?"

Maurice's reflective smile and gaze telegraphed his thoughts of younger days. "You remind me of my dear wife and I, when we were first married. The way you two look at each other and enjoy each other is electrifying. Keep that spark alive—do you hear me? Never let it fade."

As Armand and Andrea gazed at each other with warm smiles, Maurice adjusted his glasses and added, "Now, allow me to get you that address."

He spun around and walked toward his ledger. As he skimmed through the pages, he said, "As for this Alfonse Moreau fellow, I must say, he was a bit odd." He looked back at the couple. "Well, by odd I mean seriously off. You know, not too clever...and dare I say, at least according to what some of the town folks had said, a bit of a crook...and, *ah*! Here it is!"

With that, Maurice gave them the address and added, "I see here that one of the books he ordered wasn't about Leonardo." He adjusted his glasses to look closer. "It was about Christie's and Sotheby's."

Armand looked at Andrea. "Very interesting."

Andrea purchased a book on Leonardo and another entitled *The History of Art*. Then they each thanked Maurice and exited the shop.

The next day, Armand called his father to make sure he was all right. Sergio told him not to worry; it had been an anxiety attack and that his biggest problem now was his friend Paolo. His half-blind old buddy had taken on the role of nurse and was driving Sergio batty, knocking things off the table, misplacing Sergio's toothpaste and using his toothbrush to scrub the dirty dishes. Armand had to laugh, but was relieved that his father was well. He wrapped up their colorful conversation and turned his thoughts back to the investigation.

Hopping in the Renault, Armand and Andrea drove six kilometers into the rustic countryside and came upon a narrow dirt road. As a plume of dust billowed in their wake, Armand looked over at Andrea. "Are you sure this is where Rammenwadel is?"

She looked back down at the map, then at Armand. "Yes. The map shows that we're *on* Rammenwadel, and it comes to a dead end."

No sooner did she say that, than they saw a dilapidated bungalow up ahead with a broken down fence. Fastened to the fence with rusted nails was a rotted piece of wood with the address sloppily painted on it. "There," she said. "That's the house, all right."

"You mean shack," Armand said as they pulled up to the weather-beaten cabin. They pulled over on the grassy shoulder and waited for the dust cloud to pass over their vehicle. The small farm was badly neglected and only large enough to support a single family, at best. Armand knocked on the weathered door. They waited several minutes, but no answer. Andrea peered in the pitted window, but only saw a disheveled living room with a kitchen beyond that, the sink loaded with dirty dishes.

"No one's home," She said. "But someone does live here."

Armand pointed. "Let's take a peek around back."

As they walked around to the rear of the bungalow, they came upon an old man, his back toward them, irrigating a small patch of dirt with a rusted hoe.

Armand called out, "Excuse me, *Monsieur*."

The old man pivoted around, startled, as his eyes bulged. He grabbed the hoe defensively, and said in French, "Who are you? What do you want?"

Armand raised his hands gently and told Andrea to tell him they meant no harm, which she did in French. The old man couldn't speak English, so Andrea took on the role of translator.

As expected, Andrea soon learned that the old man was in indeed Alphonse Moreau. She introduced herself as Andrea Dejarnette, and her business partner as Armand Santore, aliases they had used previously on the Ghent case while posing as art dealers. She then explained how they happened to be touring France, but got lost while taking a scenic drive into the countryside.

Moreau shook his head with disappointment. "What a strange coincidence," he said, which Andrea translated for Armand.

Alphonse's wrinkled old face twisted with regret. "You see, I happened to have a painting, which I just recently learned was by Leonardo da Vinci."

Armand feigned an innocent smile. "You jest, of course? How could a man living out *here* have such a valuable possession?"

Andrea translated, as Alphonse replied, "Well, you see, I used to work for the Bugatti auto factory many years ago." He pulled out a soiled handkerchief from his rear pocket, wiped his running nose, then shoved it back in. "It was during the war when Ettore Bugatti gave it to me for safekeeping. You know, to hide it from those damn Nazis." The man's face suddenly flushed with suspicion, as he said, "*You're* not Nazis, are you?"

Andrea almost laughed and assured him they weren't, as the man sighed and continued, "Anyhow, *Monsieur* Bugatti said if or when he should die, the painting would be mine."

As Andrea translated, Armand tried to conceal his smirk. "Why would Ettore Bugatti simply *give you* a precious painting?"

Alphonse leaned on his hoe like a cane, his feeble body struggling to stay erect. "*Monsieur* Santore, he liked me very much. That's why. And when his favorite son Jean died, he was terribly distraught...and well, he sort of took me under his wing...as a young brother, I suppose."

Armand just nodded, taking in all the manure Moreau was shoveling while cordially keeping a straight face. "Ah, so I see," he said. "So, if Ettore generously gave you a valuable Leonardo..." Armand's head spun around to view the dilapidated bungalow and rundown farm, then back at *Monsieur* Moreau. "How is it that you never sold it to make a fortune? You could have been living in a mansion and living the good life."

Moreau's face twisted with humiliation upon hearing Andrea's translation. Exasperated, he sat down on a tree stump, and looked up at Armand. "I never knew it was a da Vinci, *Monsieur* Santore, until two months ago." Again, he pulled out his hanky and wiped his runny nose. He rested the soiled cloth on his tattered pants. "As you can see, I'm not a cultured man. I just loved the painting for its beauty." He shook his head, mad at himself and the world. "Besides,

Ettore never told me who painted it or how valuable it was. I suppose I'm not too bright, either, *Monsieur*, because I did sell it, just last week."

Armand and Andrea's eyes widened, as Armand exclaimed, "Sold it!? To whom? And for how much?"

Moreau gazed at the ground and shook his head. "I sold it to a man named Kurt Heinmann or Hoffburgh or something like that." He looked back up. "I'm not good with names. He offered me 24,000 francs."

Armand's eyes rolled. "Jesus! *Monsieur* Moreau, that's only around $4,000 US dollars. That's chicken feed."

Alphonse nodded solemnly. "Perhaps, but you see, once I found out I had a da Vinci, I couldn't find any buyers. I even contacted Christie's and Sotheby's. They didn't believe me and thought I was a lunatic." He looked around his depressing property, then back at Armand. "Two fellas even drove up here, but turned around once they laid eyes on my abode. To hell with them all!" He blustered. "I loathe the rich. They're all a bunch of greedy snobs. They pay men like me spit to work and slave their lives away, and then they come here and look down their haughty noses at me like I'm a feral dog! I'm just trying to survive, damn it!"

He reached into his tattered shirt pocket and pulled out a wrinkled old photo. "My beautiful eighteen-year-old daughter, Claudette, had died because I couldn't pay for her operation, and soon after, my wife left me. That was many years ago, but the pain remains." Tears welled in his eyes as he gritted the few remaining teeth in his baldhead. "And that son of a bitch, Kurt, shafted me, too! The bastard took off with the painting and only gave me the 10,000 francs deposit. He hasn't returned my phone calls, and he's nowhere to be found. I'm sick of being shit upon!" He looked up toward the heavens and cried, "Do you hear me up there!? I'm damn sick and tired of it! Take me! Take me now!"

Armand and Andrea's heads lowered. They had heard all the rumors of Alphonse Moreau being odd, slow, strange, a thief, and a liar, but the conditions that caused those attributes were never understood. Not that it condoned Moreau's illegal or immoral actions, but Armand and Andrea now at least recognized the complicated and tragic life Alphonse had to endure.

As Armand looked at the pathetic image of Alphonse Moreau his revulsion simmered to disappointment with a touch of sympathy. He stepped closer and put his arm around the weeping old man. "Alphonse, where did you first meet Kurt?"

Moreau wiped his runny nose once again and looked up at Armand through his cataract-clad eyes. Upon hearing Andrea's translation, he replied, "I happened to see him passing through town—Molsheim, that is—fairly regularly." He scratched his wrinkled forehead. "But we first made contact in *Maurice's Librairie d'art* two months ago. I was buying some books and we struck up a conversation. That's when he told me he was an art dealer. However, I first wanted to see if I could sell the painting on my own to Sotheby's or Christie's. But when that fell through, I contacted Kurt." He glanced back at the house. "That's when we met *right there*. You see, I kept the painting in my attic, and well, we did the exchange on a gentlemen's handshake. But he hasn't answered my calls since."

As Armand huffed, Alphonse shrugged. "What can I say? That's the way I was brought up, *Monsieur* Santore. But there's no integrity anymore."

"So, you have no contract, no bill of sale, nothing? No full name or address of this man named Kurt written down?"

Alphonse's shoulders sank like a scolded child. "What do you want from me? I told you before, I reckon I'm not too bright."

"*Not too bright!*" Armand huffed. "That would insinuate you had some level of brightness, Alphonse. Christ! You've stumbled through life in total darkness!" Armand immediately looked at Andrea. "*Don't* translate that!" He shook his head; annoyed that some people go through life without applying themselves, then complain when their lot in life isn't a bowl of cherries. Yet, he wasn't sure if Alphonse was a lazy deadbeat or truly slow, the former deserving his ire, the latter sympathy. But what truly sparked Armand's frustration was that another lead was so close yet drastically so far. *Who could this Kurt Heinmann or Hoffburgh, or whatever the hell his real name is, possibly be?* He thought. *And* where *could he possibly be?*

He looked at Andrea. "He said this guy Kurt disappeared, but had frequented Molsheim in the past. Ask him why, for what reason?"

As Andrea relayed Armand's query, Alphonse rubbed his stubbly chin and gently shook his head. "I don't recall," he mumbled, lost in his own grief.

Armand looked at Andrea and frowned, when Alphonse suddenly looked up at Armand. "*Une minute!*" he exclaimed, as his milky cataracts rolled with thought. "I believe Kurt said...well, at least *I think* he said...something about a storage facility, somewhere nearby. *Oui,* that's it! A storage facility, for his artwork." He scratched his baldhead, as his excited voice withered to a dejected utterance: "But, I'm very sorry. I don't recall if he ever mentioned where."

As Armand received the translation he looked at Andrea. "Well, we can't win them all. But there *is* a silver lining. Eventually we'll have to run into con man, Kurt. And who knows what other goodies the shyster is peddling."

Armand and Andrea spent another two days surveilling Molsheim with no sign of the mystery man. Discouraged but optimistic, they made the best of the situation, making their impromptu honeymoon/hunt an enjoyable endeavor by taking in the sights. They visited *Musée de la Chartreuse*, a monastery turned into an art museum, featuring works by Veronese, Le Brun, Chardin and others, and spent a relaxing evening at the *Domaine Boehler* vineyard sampling wines and engaging in conversations with locals and travelers.

The next morning Andrea sat in their hotel-room bed reading her book on Leonardo, when Armand strolled out of the bathroom, clean-shaven, hair combed, and ready to roll. "Okay, sweetie, put the book down, the day is wasting away." He walked over and ran his fingers under her buttocks. "In fact, I think you're growing roots." He spun his head around playfully. "Where are the pruning shears? I need to cut you loose."

Andrea laughed as she peered at the clock. "Honey, it's only 7:03. I've only been reading for fifteen minutes. We're on our honeymoon, so why the rush?"

Armand slipped his tweed jacket over his turtleneck sweater. "Because, if you'll recall, Peaches, *you* took us on this detour from our *planned* honeymoon. So this is still the Case of the Lost *Leda*, my dear. So, hop to it!" he said with a playful smile.

Andrea chuckled and put the book down. "Very well, Sherlock. But where are we off to in such a hurry?"

"Fort de Mutzig."

"A fort!" Andrea balked. "That sounds like another historical landmark that you love dragging me to. That's *not* work, Sherlock."

"Well, Watson, you see, you have yet to comprehend the analytical mind of a sleuth. I happened to learn an interesting bit of local history last night from Victor; he's the fellow I was talking to at the vineyard. He informed me that the Germans had built Fort de Mutzig just prior to World War One, when this territory was under their domain. Originally named Fort Kaiser Wilhelm II, it happens to be the first and largest fortification built of poured concrete, and it features twenty-two huge artillery turrets *and* underground passageways with ventilation. It was a marvel in its day and I was told that it has survived in surprisingly good condition."

"That's just swell," Andrea moaned. "So, what does *that* have to do with this case?"

Armand slipped his false identification in his wallet and said, "Well, that's where the art of deduction comes into play, my dear Watson. You see, the Germans, and the Nazis in particular, were notorious for their bunkers. Not only did they lie in wait there to kill enemy forces, or, like Hitler, hide like rats, but that's also where they stored some of their looted artwork. And with this Kurt fellow being German and having a storage facility somewhere nearby, I believe it's very likely that he's using the fort's underground bunkers."

Andrea's beautifully arched eyebrows inverted in thought. "Well, Sherlock. Aren't you overlooking something? How could a crook like Kurt hide paintings in a busy public museum?"

"Simple, my dear Watson. Because it's not a museum. It's defunct, has been since the war. However, Victor said there are plans to renovate it and turn it into a museum. And that not only makes the *Mutzig Fort* a great place to hide stolen artwork, but with news of it being renovated, Kurt will have to start moving all his artwork to another location. That's *if* he hasn't done so already. So, time *is* of the essence."

A smile of admiration enlivened Andrea's face. "I think you might very well be smarter than Sherlock. My apologies, sweetheart."

"No apologies necessary, it's only an educated hunch. But let's see if it pans out." Armand slipped off his wedding band. "Are you ready to go, Andrea Dejarnette?"

She nodded and hurriedly got dressed, then slipped off her engagement and wedding rings. "Ready, Armand Santore!"

Some twenty minutes later, they drove up a hill along an abandoned dirt path. In the distance they could see the immense fortress embedded into the mountainside. As they approached, the intimidating turrets and thick concrete walls, which partially protruded out of the soil, evoked an ominous aura, one of utter dread and massive deadly power. Armand felt as if they were stepping back in time, as visions of the two World Wars came vividly into focus.

Off to the side, almost buried in the woods, Andrea spotted a Volkswagen bus and a brand new 1985 Mercedes. "Armand! Look over there! Someone's here."

Armand pulled up to one of the fortress's entranceways and came to a stop. He pointed to the glove compartment. "I put a thirty-eight revolver in there, just in case you need it." With that, he stepped out of the Renault, shut the door, and peered in the driver's window. "Stay here. Let me see who's in there first. I have no way of knowing if these guys are harmless art thieves or professional gangsters. I'll call you if everything seems copasetic. Otherwise, if trouble brews, don't be afraid to use it."

"I don't want to stay here," she whined. "I'm coming with you."

"Andrea! I'm not being Mr. Macho here. This is just sensible strategy. I need a backup if things go wrong. As I told you, I called my buddies in Interpol. Lou Gaspard and a few agents should arrive sometime soon. But if, by some stroke of bad luck, these goons have guns and, well…you protect yourself. Got it?"

Andrea smirked. "Why aren't *you* carrying a gun?"

"I'm approaching them as an art dealer, not a gun dealer. If they frisk me, that would only jeopardize the whole operation. Besides, it's not my style. I prefer talking my way out of jambs. Now, are we clear?"

"Clear. But aren't you going to kiss me good-bye?"

Armand chuckled. "I don't expect to be gone long, and, let's face it, it wouldn't look too good if I walk in there with lipstick on my face." As Andrea chuckled, he continued, "Anyhow, I doubt there will be any trouble. If they didn't rough up or kill Alphonse, it's unlikely that they're armed thugs. I'm just giving you this rundown to be prepared for any situation that arises. Now, are you ready, *Mademoiselle* Dejarnette?"

Andrea pouted. "Well, I don't like not being married to you anymore, but yes, *Monsieur* Santore. I'm ready." As Armand started to walk away, she added "And you better be careful!"

"I will," he said with a smile, as he walked toward the massive structure. Andrea watched intently while her pulse beat faster with each step Armand took. As he passed through the concrete threshold and disappeared into the fortress, she took a deep breath and tried to calm her nerves.

Inside, Armand pulled out his flashlight and started to walk down a dark, narrow passageway. The tunnel was oval shaped and fashioned out of large elongated bricks with random tunnels branching off the main trunk. Armand could sense he was traveling deeper underground with each step and with each added drop of moisture that accumulated on his skin. He covered his nose to avoid the dank smell, when suddenly a figure sprung out of the shadows, a luger in the man's hand. "*Halt! Wer bist du?*" the man barked in German.

Armand recoiled. "Hold on, pal!" he said. "I don't speak German." He motioned with his hand. "*Put down* the gun!"

The burly man, with a crew cut and a round, rock-like face, kept the gun pointed at Armand, and demanded in English, "*I said*, who are you?"

"My name is Armand Santore. I'm an art dealer on vacation with my partner. She's outside and can easily call the police if she hears a shot. So, put down the gun, I'm not armed."

"But I am," the man said gruffly. "And I'll decide when or *if* I'll lower it. Now shut up and show me your identification."

Armand slipped his false identification out and showed the thug, who looked like Ernst Röhm, with a mustache and scar on his face to boot. Convinced, the stocky man relaxed his grip but still held the gun pointed at Armand's stomach. "My name is Erich Bormann. Sorry for the security check, but we handle expensive artifacts down here. But the real question is; how did *you*, an *art dealer* no less, find out about us?"

Armand clutched the metal flashlight tighter as he said, "Actually, I came across an old-timer, a bit of a deadbeat, trying to sell a da Vinci. I believe you know him—Alphonse Moreau."

Erich gripped his gun tighter and raised it up. "If you're here to collect that old fool's balance, you've made a big mistake, *Herr* Santore."

Armand laughed, playing up his bad boy image. "Of course not. Like I said, the man is a loser. I'm not here to collect for him, I'm here because I have a very rich client who would love that painting, and he'll pay handsomely for it. Certainly a lot more than 4,000 US dollars. Or should I say, 1,000 dollars."

Erich smirked. "What makes you think we don't already have a buyer?"

"I really don't care who you have lined up, Erich. I guarantee that my buyer will beat any price you can get on the black market. Fencing a da Vinci is the most difficult transaction to accomplish in the art world. That's *if*, you're dealing with smart and affluent clients who have stringent verification tests and can afford to pay top dollar, which mine are. And of course, that's *if* the painting is even authentic, which I doubt."

"Of course it's real!" Erich snapped. "My boss is no fool."

Just then, a figure emerged from an adjacent tunnel. "Of course I'm no fool!" the tall middle-aged man snapped.

"Nor am I, Kurt," Armand replied promptly.

Kurt glared at Erich. "Why did you tell this man my name?"

"He didn't," Armand interjected.

Armand explained the same story to Kurt and then expounded on his impressive, yet fictitious, resume, along with boasting about some of his underhanded escapades in the black market.

Kurt smiled, he appreciated that Armand had no interest in Alphonse Moreau and had eminent contacts. He felt he was in good company, and said, "Well, you might very well be useful. I'd like to show you some of my collection, Armand. Most of it has been transported already, since we can no longer use this facility," his head turned toward the tunnel, "but I still have two Klimts here, along with several Monets, a splendid Botticelli, one Crivelli, and a Titian." He looked back, deep into Armand's eyes, his demeanor unnervingly serious, dead serious. "Actually, I'd like to test your expertise."

Unruffled, Armand replied, "My expertise lies in the Renaissance and Baroque masters, Kurt. So I can certainly assess the last three you mentioned, but not the others."

"Very well, follow me." Kurt nodded to Erich, indicating he should follow behind Armand, with his gun still drawn.

As the threesome walked down the dark tunnel with their flashlights, they eventually came upon a rusted ironclad door. As they passed over the threshold, they entered a huge underground chamber, equipped with low UV fluorescent lights, and an HVAC system that controlled the humidity and temperature. Lined up on easels were all the paintings Kurt had mentioned.

Armand walked over to the Botticelli. He scrutinized Sandro's slick hard edges and vibrant palette of colors. He shook his head in amazement. "This is spectacular!" He peered back at Kurt. "You have a gem here."

Kurt smiled. "Indeed I do! Good work."

Armand walked over to the Crivelli. Again, his eyes analyzed the brushstrokes, the stiff, doll-like human figures, the sharp lines of the buildings, and Carlo's experimental, but flawed, use of perspective. Again, Armand turned and looked at Kurt, amazed. "I don't know how you came across these. But this one is also original. Very impressive."

"I'm glad you like my collection, Armand." Kurt pointed to the Titian. "Now, take a good look at my favorite of the three, and feast your eyes!"

Armand stepped in front of the Titian. He looked only briefly and said, "Ah, *The Aldobrandini Madonna*. A very nice piece!" He turned toward Kurt. "But it hangs in the National Gallery in London. This, I'm afraid, is a fake."

Kurt smiled as he placed his flashlight down and clapped tepidly. "Bravo! You did well, Armand." He paused a second, then asked, "I didn't get your last name?"

"Santore," Armand replied as he walked toward him. "And I never got yours?"

Kurt squinted as he extended his hand to shake. "Hoffmann, Kurt Hoffmann." As they shook, Armand's eyes wavered in thought, while Kurt said, "Santore? How come I know that name?"

A chill went down Armand's back as bad memories flooded his head. Meanwhile, Andrea suddenly appeared at the entrance, as all three men pivoted with surprise. Erich aimed his gun at her, while Armand barked, "Put the damn gun down, Erich, she's with me!"

Erich looked over at Kurt, who nodded. "Easy, Erich." He looked at Andrea. "And what is your name, *Fraulein*?"

Before she could speak, Kurt interjected, *"No!* Let me guess." He glanced at Armand, then back at her. "Just as your partner, Armand Santore, is an expert on Renaissance paintings, *I* am an expert on names. Could your name be Andrea Dejarnette?"

Baffled, Andrea looked quizzically at Armand, whose face flushed.

Kurt barked, "Erich, point the gun at *Herr* Santore! *Mach Schnell!"*

As Erich complied, Kurt looked at Armand. "You filthy dog! Did you think I could ever forget the names of the man who killed my father, and his bitch accomplice? How dare you come here and show your faces to me, to *me!"*

Armand's worst nightmare had materialized as a chill ran down his back. The dark memory of confronting Kurt's father, Gerard Hoffmann, during his Russian Link case came screaming back into his mind, as he retorted, "I did *not* kill your father, Kurt, he took his own life—with cyanide."

Rage enlivened Kurt's face as he blasted, "Do you think he would have done that if not for *you*!? You treacherous snake! Don't test my patience with semantics, Armand Santore! If you came here to kill me, you're mistaken. You'll only find your own tomb here, you pig!"

As Erich kept his luger trained on Armand, adrenaline rushed through his veins, while Armand replied, "I had no idea you were behind this operation, Kurt. It was a freak coincidence. Now listen to me; I know the papers had mentioned I cooperated with Interpol to break up your father's art ring, but that wasn't true. I was looking to start a working relationship with your father. He killed himself when Interpol arrived. Fortunately, I managed to con them into thinking that I headed that sting. That's what boosted my image in the papers as a hero and a first-rate art dealer. That's why *I* have contacts that you could *never* attain, Kurt. I'm in it for the money, plain and simple. And I'm interested in Leonardo's *Leda and the Swan*, that's all. So, let's keep our cool." Now with Andrea in the mix, Armand encountered a new dynamic—an almost heart-stopping need to protect the woman he loved. "I can make you very, very rich if you'll sell it to my buyer, Kurt. We're all here to make money, no one needs to go to prison for murder. So tell Erich to put down the gun."

As Kurt's face radiated doubt mixed with a gut feeling of hatred, Andrea furtively put her hand behind her back, while Armand continued his peace negotiations. "Kurt, listen to me. I know you'll never get what I can for the Leda. Clear your head of the lies about me, and I'll get you top dollar that only major auction houses get. I'm talking about 400 million dollars, Kurt. You can't even get a fraction of that on the black market with shady clients. So just tell me where you have it?"

Kurt glared at Armand, his soothing words all made sense but the voice in Kurt's gut was telling him otherwise. For years he had lived with the pain and horror of his father's tragic death and Armand's one-minute-long plea of innocence just wasn't cutting through the thick layers of pent-up vengeance. Kurt finally spat, "I don't believe you! You'll *never* lay eyes on it, do you hear me? *Never!*"

"If it's not here," Armand said calmly, maintaining his con, "I'm sure you have it stored safely somewhere nearby. Perhaps just an hour or two away?"

"Perhaps you're wrong, you murdering maggot, it's a good six hours away. So, it's time to say good-bye!" With that, Kurt signaled to Erich, who pulled the trigger!

A bullet tore through Armand's chest as Andrea screamed and pulled out the thirty-eight from behind her back. Erich's eyes bulged as a loud *pop*! echoed, the bullet boring a hole in Erich's stomach. Erich dropped the gun and grabbed his bleeding belly, while Kurt scurried to retrieve the pistol. Before he could pick it up, Armand smashed him from behind with the metal flashlight, knocking his jaw clear out of its socket, along with two teeth, and twisting his head sideways.

Armand grabbed the luger and pointed it at Kurt, who rose unsteadily to his feet, moaning and spitting blood as he held his broken jaw.

Meanwhile, Andrea tried to collect herself as she kept her gun pointed at Erich. Her mouth was dry and her hand shook as she worriedly looked at Armand. "Are you all right?"

With one hand on his wound and the other still clutching the luger, he said, "Not sure. It just feels like someone punched me near the shoulder."

Erich wobbled and fell to the floor, unconscious, while Kurt cussed Armand, as blood spurted from his mouth.

Just then, six Interpol agents stormed into the bunker. Louis Gaspard looked at Armand. "Sorry we're late."

"So am I," Armand said, while another agent called an ambulance. Two others administered smelling salt to awaken Erich, then bandaged his stomach, while another agent wrapped up Armand's chest wound.

Fifteen minutes later, two ambulances arrived. Erich and Kurt were carted away in one vehicle, while Andrea found herself riding in the back of another with Armand, her head still in a daze and her nerves tingling with anxiety. She looked at him and shook her head. "This is terrible: you being shot, another dead end, and...and, oh dear, I can't believe I shot someone."

"I'm so sorry it came to that," Armand said, his voice marred with regret. "I was expecting Lou Gaspard and his fellow agents to arrive sooner to handle any possible dirty work. I had no idea I'd run into Kurt Hoffmann. What horrible luck."

Andrea looked at him with moist eyes. "Well, I just couldn't wait around any longer. It's a good thing I came when I did. If I waited for Interpol you'd probably be d-dead," she said with a frazzled stutter.

Armand rubbed his aching wound. "That's very possible. I'll be fine. But we make a darn good team, sweetheart."

Andrea chuckled nervously. "*Good* team!? Really?" she said as she glanced at his wound. "You almost were killed." Tears finally broke free and streamed down her face. "I'm not sure I can handle this."

Armand reached over and lovingly grasped her hand. "Sure you can. You handled the situation perfectly. You had the gut instinct to move when the situation called for it. You're better than any field partner I had when I worked at the FBI." He looked deeply in to her magnetic eyes. "No lie." As she smiled, he admitted, "Well, actually, I didn't have any field partners in the FBI, only desk agents digging up intel." As she laughed nervously, he added, "But you really were magnificent, sweetheart. And this case has made great headway ever since you had me stop at Maurice's bookshop."

Andrea's smile withered. "How can you say that? We just ran into another brick wall. Kurt never revealed where he hid *Leda*."

Armand smiled. "I guess it will come in time, but you need to listen more carefully, sweetheart. During my last exchange with Kurt, I lured him to reveal information that might offer us a clue."

Perplexed, Andrea tried to recall their conversation. Her eyes wandered and her nervous brain churned, but still she couldn't recall anything remotely useful.

As the ambulance pulled up to the hospital, Armand said, "I got Kurt to reveal that the *Leda* is stored six hours away from Molsheim."

Andrea shook her head. "What good is that? That's still an awfully vast area, Armand. Talk about a needle lost in a sprawling haystack."

Just then, the rescue crew grabbed Armand's gurney and started to wheel him into the emergency room. Andrea scurried up alongside, as Armand replied, "All we need to do is draw a circle around Molsheim on the map with a six-hour radius."

As they rolled him into the operating room, Andrea said, "I still don't see how that helps, sweetheart?"

A nurse stopped Andrea as the doors started to close before them.

Andrea yelled out, "I love you!"

"And I you," came Armand's fading reply.

Three hours later, Armand and Andrea sat in the recovery room with a map sprawled out on the bed before them. Armand made a makeshift compass with a piece of string and a pencil. He pressed one end of the string down on Molsheim with his finger and extended the string six hours away (based on the speed limit), then drew a circle. The pencil passed over several major cities and neighboring countries, as Andrea pouted. "You see what I mean, it can be anywhere."

Armand continued undaunted as the pencil passed clockwise over the cities of Amsterdam, Leipzig, Prague, Turin, and Amboise.

Armand nearly laughed with glee. "Bingo!" He looked at her. "You see, I told you I pulled a clue out of Kurt's crooked mouth. This is even better than I hoped for. He gave me the exact location."

Andrea scratched her temple. "But you targeted *five* major cities, each in different countries, no less?"

"Yes," he said. "But only one makes perfect sense."

Perplexedly, she looked back down at the map, as Armand said, "You've been reading up on Leonardo, sweetheart. Think!"

Suddenly it clicked. "Oh! Yes, of course!" she exclaimed as her eyes lit up, then darted at her brilliant husband. "Amboise, France. That's where da Vinci was buried."

"Exactly," Armand said.

As the doctor walked in, Armand slipped on his shoes and said, "Make it quick, Doc, because I'm checking out."

"Oh, no you're not!" the doctor demanded, while sticking a stethoscope on his chest. "You're staying here for observation."

"Well, jot this observation down, Doc, as I walk out the door. Because we're leaving!" With that, Armand grasped Andrea's hand and they exited the room, the treasure map clutched in Andrea's other hand.

Before leaving the hospital, however, Armand stormed into Kurt's room, who looked up from his bed in shock, his mouth clamped and wired.

"I just wanted to stop by to thank you, Kurt."

Kurt's swollen, purple lips furled with venom, as Armand said, "My partner and I are heading to Amboise right now to collect *Leda*." Armand smiled. "Da Vinci's tomb, how thoughtful of you."

Kurt's eyes widened with surprise as his face turned into a snarling portrait of disdain. He grabbed his aching, wired jaw and growled through his clenched teeth, "How!? How d-did you…f-find out!?"

"Never mind that," Armand replied. "It's all over for you, Kurt. So, since you'll be losing your prized *Leda*, you might as well tell me why you chose to hide it in Leonardo's tomb?"

Kurt petulantly turned his head away, as a huff of humiliation hissed out of his metal mouth. Heatedly, he looked back at his nemesis. "You're t-the brilliant s-sleuth, S-Santore. F-Figure it out!"

Armand smiled. "Actually, I believe I did, that's *if* you're a true art lover. Judging by your father's obsession, I imagine he instilled at least that much goodness in your rotten head. I just wanted to hear it from your own mouth, but I see that's wired shut. What a pity."

"Very f-funny…you p-pig!" Kurt spat through his clenched teeth. "S-so now w-what? You're… an art ex-p-pert…*and* a m-mind reader? Is t-that it?"

"Well, I just hope your reasoning for storing it in Leonardo's sacred tomb has a deeper meaning, Kurt. After all, da Vinci was viewed as almost a god among men. And since Leonardo's unique take on the Leda myth was that she made love to a god to bequeath to the world offspring of divine beauty, I'm wondering if you placed Leda with Leonardo, the man-god, with the hopes that Leonardo's divine offspring—namely his painting that's been lost for centuries—will be bestowed upon the world."

Kurt quasi-nodded, grudgingly, as he grabbed his aching jaw. "M-my intentions...w-weren't *t-that* complex...or p-poetic. B-but, yes, it w-was done...with s-sincere respect." He paused briefly, as old memories filled his aching head, then continued, "My f-father...and Goering...m-may have d-dealt with s-stolen art...but t-they had a d-deep love...and appreciation... f-for t-these artists and t-their w-works, which...t-they instilled...in m-me." He paused to mitigate the pain in his broken jaw by sipping cold water through a straw, then continued, "I'm s-sure you know...m-many f-forgeries...hang in m-museums. So, I t-truly wanted...L-Leonardo's *Leda* to m-make it...into a m-museum. Because it *is*...that s-special." He took another sip of water to sooth his parched and swollen throat, and added, "And t-that *dummkopf*, M-Moreau...kept that m-masterpiece...in his attic...for f-four decades. I even gave t-that...m-moron 10,000 francs...which is m-more...than he d-deserved. So, I ain't all that b-bad, Armand."

"If that's the case, Kurt," Armand lifted up the large keychain he seized from the Mutzig bunker before being carted off to the hospital. "Then tell me, which key is it? Not that I couldn't simply try them all once there, but just to show good faith, tell me, it might help soften your prison sentence."

After a brief moment of silence, Kurt finally complied, and even explained exactly where and how to access the hidden vault.

Just then, an Interpol guard posted by the door leaned in. "*Monsieur* Arnolfini, the doctor is heading this way, best you leave at once."

Kurt looked at Armand. "Arnolfini? I t-thought...your n-name...was Santore? Are you e-even...an art d-dealer?"

Armand shrugged. "Figure it out."

With that, Armand and Andrea slipped out of the hospital. They hopped in their rented Renault and drove westward through the scenic countryside of France, even stopping to eat lunch. Several hours later, they arrived at Amboise.

Up ahead, they could see the impressive Château Royal d'Amboise—the sprawling mansion of Leonardo's patron, King Francis I. As they drove closer, Armand peered over at the small, but architecturally exquisite, Chapel of Saint-Hubert.

"There it is! Leonardo's resting place," Armand said, as he parked the car.

Reverently, they walked slowly toward the edifice, as Andrea said, "I've always wondered why so many of his paintings ended up in the Louvre." She peered at Armand. "Having spent the last three years of his life here certainly gave France a few gems. Personally, I love *The Virgin and Child with Saint Anne*. Yet, I'm not sure what to make of his *Saint John the Baptist*. It's a bit ambiguous."

Armand nodded. "Yes, I agree on both accounts. And of course, France has Leonardo's pièce de résistance, the *Mona Lisa*. I see you're becoming a pro on the old master."

Andrea smiled. "Not quite, but I am getting to know Leonardo better. He was far more complex than I ever imagined."

Armand nodded, knowing that Leonardo was certainly the most enigmatic, multifaceted, and prophetic of his elite peers. He also knew that despite da Vinci being viewed primarily as an artist, the fact was, he was equally hired as a theatrical impresario, military engineer, and a city planner, among a myriad of other endeavors, including being an outstanding musician, who even invented instruments and won a competition.

Andrea grasped Armand's hand, while Armand smiled with reflecting wonder. "Yes, Leonardo was truly a magnificent being. And come to think of it, the world is still very lucky if only being aware of his art." He looked into her eyes. "I think a great artist is just as important as a farmer. While one feeds the stomach, the other feeds the soul. And Leonardo certainly gave civilization much nourishment."

With a warm smile from Andrea, Armand crossed himself as they entered the sacred chapel. They walked up to the wrought iron railing, which stood in front of the marble, tomb-slab embedded in the tile floor. It featured a round bronze medallion with the likeness of the master, along with his name below that in capital letters.

Reverently, they each bowed their heads and offered prayers. Armand could feel a wave of emotions soaring through him as he thanked God for gifting the world with such a man, a man who not only defined his era but also miraculously envisioned *and* documented a plethora of ingenious inventions and discoveries, many of which only came to fruition hundreds of years later.

Andrea crossed herself, then looked at Armand. "Do you think we're actually looking at Leonardo's remains?"

Armand nodded. *"I* truly believe so," he said, well aware of the disjointed journey da Vinci's bones had taken.

Having originally been entombed in the church of St. Florentin in Amboise, per his wishes, Leonardo's death was enshrouded in mystery, mirroring his enigmatic life. The St. Florentin church had unfortunately been destroyed during the French Revolution. However, in 1863, Arsene Houssaye excavated the ruinous site and believed he uncovered Leonardo's bones, as well as fragments of his tombstone. Several years later, the remains were moved to the Chapel of Saint-Hubert, with one eyewitness stating that the skull was unusually large, hence proving to be the former domicile of da Vinci's enormous intellect. Meanwhile, several skeptics claimed that Houssaye's discovery was inconclusive.

Armand's head spun around, seeking the secret panel Kurt had mentioned. "There it is!" he said, as he crossed himself and then walked over to the marble panel. With the manipulation of a barely visible lever, Armand swiveled it open. Before him stood a bronze door. Armand excitedly inserted the key and *presto!* The door creaked open.

Armand and Andrea took deep breaths, entered the narrow opening, then descended down the stone-carved, spiral staircase. As they did, they could feel the presence of fresh, meticulously controlled air. Moments later, they reached the bottom and entered a dark vault. Armand blindly searched the wall and located the switch. With bated breath, Armand flipped the toggle.

In a wondrous glow of illumination, Leonardo's magnificent *Leda and the Swan* stood before them in all its glory. Tears mounted in Armand's eyes as he clenched his fists, hoping fervently that the apparition before him was authentic. Humbly, he walked toward the alluring painting as his heart beat with titillating flutters of emotion. His eyes drank in its beauty as if a 300 thousand dollar bottle of 1947 Cheval Blanc, his face turning equally white, drunk with admiration. His body trembled as he leaned in closer. He had to see if he could locate one of the clearest indications of a genuine Leonardo—fingerprints.

The Italian master was unique in that during the process of inventing the art of *sfumato*—namely, slightly blurring the unnaturally hard edges used to outline the human form—Leonardo used his fingers to smudge the paint, adding a whole new dimension of realism to his paintings and influencing countless others who followed. Of equal importance, Leonardo had inadvertently or intentionally left behind his precious fingerprints for posterity.

Armand almost fainted as a wave of utter bliss washed over him, his eyes blinking hard to see if what his mind was processing was just his wishful imagination or the actual fingerprints of the Renaissance genius, the man who fired Armand's imagination ever since a child. It was almost a moment of spiritual transcendence as Armand's love and admiration communed with the lofty spirit of da Vinci, whose name means *win*. And on all accounts, Armand felt like he won the grandest of all prizes.

Excitedly, he spun around and looked at Andrea. "Dear Lord! By all visible indications, this masterpiece *is* authentic."

Andrea stepped closer and embraced him, tightly. "You did it!" She planted a loving kiss on his lips, then leaned back. "This truly *is* a momentous day. What a honeymoon!"

Armand chuckled. "Indeed!" He looked at the alluring and naked *Leda*, then back at Andrea. "I'm in the presence of two paragons of beauty. And standing beside the remains of the art world's quintessential genius. Dear Lord, it doesn't get better than this!"

"Actually, it can," Andrea said. "I've been waiting for the right moment to tell you, and this is surely it. I found out this morning—I'm pregnant."

Armand's face lit up as his heart seemed to soar into the lofty heavens. He gazed down at her stomach and lovingly rubbed it, feeling as if the swan god himself. "This truly is a picture of utter perfection!"

Andrea smiled. "And your father will be delighted."

Armand chuckled. "Indeed he will. The Arnolfini clan *will* survive."

With that, the newlyweds entwined in a warm embrace, as each peeked at the luminous *Leda* as they kissed.

THE CARPEAUX CAPER

Two days after celebrating the glorious return of Leonardo's *Leda*, accompanied by a litany of press releases and media mayhem, Armand and Andrea were sitting at a curbside table at Renate's Café on the Champs-Élysées enjoying the tail end of their official honeymoon.

Just then, Louis Gaspard from Interpol walked up to their table. "Do you mind if I join you?"

Armand glanced up. "Not at all, Lou, have a seat."

As Louis sat down, Armand looked at Andrea. "You remember Lou, right?"

Andrea nodded. "Yes. How can I forget," she said, barely concealing her discontent at his arriving too late to prevent her husband from being shot.

Louis noticed and lowered his head. "I apologize, Andrea." He looked up at Armand. "But your husband is alive and well, at least for now."

Armand squinted. "What do you mean *for now*?"

Louis leaned back in his chair and crossed his arms. "Well, this should come as no surprise, Armand. Claude De Ville filed a lawsuit against you and will be dragging your ass into court. He's pissed, and claims you stole his lovely *Leda*."

Armand sighed with relief. "Oh, I thought you had something *really* bad to tell me, Lou. I'm not afraid of that buffoon or his billions. I've had rich men and their top legal firms after my hide before, and Claude is no different. He'll never win in court once I present my side of the story, namely the fact that his relatives stole the masterpiece and held it hostage for five centuries, with Claude being just the last greedy captor in line."

Louis waved down a *garcon* and ordered an espresso, then leaned forward. "Okay, so I'm glad you're not surprised about Claude De *Villain*, Armand. But perhaps *this* will surprise you. While interrogating your busted-jaw buddy, Kurt Hoffmann, I learned that a French art dealer, named Pierre Dubuffet, was looking to pawn off an unknown statuette by Jean-Baptiste Carpeaux."

Armand's eyes lit up. He was well acquainted with Carpeaux's work, especially his masterful statue group *Ugolino and His Sons*, which he viewed almost monthly when visiting the Metropolitan Museum of Art. Carpeaux's *Ugolino and His Sons* was a triumph of visceral intensity, giving life to a tragic vision from Dante's *Inferno*. It was based on the imprisoned Count Ugolino and his sons, who were starved and driven mad by hunger. In desperation, Ugolino devoured his sons; a crime he would be forced to repeat for all eternity in the darkest corner of Dante's hellish allegory.

Armand's curiosity was piqued. "So, Lou, did Kurt say what this statuette was, or what it looked like?"

As the *garcon* handed Louis his espresso, he took a sip, puckered his lips, and replied nonchalantly, "Don't know, don't care." Leaning back, he added, "You know Interpol has little interest in art crimes. Your old buddies in Italy have the largest art crime force on the planet, not us."

Armand nodded irritably. "Yes, I know. I had tried to get the FBI to emulate the *Carabinieri*, but they, too, have little interest in art crimes. That's why I went out on my own."

Andrea chimed in, "Honey, we're set to go home in two days. That doesn't leave much time to start another investigation."

"True," Armand said, as he looked back at Gaspard. "Do you really think Kurt was telling the truth, or trying to send you on a wild goose chase?"

"I think Kurt will say anything to save his butt from being fondled in prison," Louis said, to a round of giggles.

Armand looked back at Andrea. "Listen, sweetie, this might be worth a look if Pierre Dubuffet lives locally." He looked back at Gaspard. "Does he?"

Louis nodded, took another sip of his espresso and said, "*Oui*. Pierre happens to have a penny-ante art gallery right here in Paris, and from what my sources say, he sells both, originals and fakes. So, there's no way of knowing if this statuette is a phony or not." He glanced at Andrea and smiled. "You might want to go home with your new bride, Arnolfini, and engage in other activities, perhaps one that's more *productive*."

As the newlyweds glanced at each other and smiled, Andrea said, "Too late, Louis. I'm already pregnant."

As Gaspard's eyes widened, Armand said, "Therefore, I'll take Dubuffet's address, Lou."

An hour later, Armand and Andrea pulled up to Pierre Dubuffet's art gallery. The sign above the door was weathered and peeling, while the displays in the picture window were lackluster at best. The couple walked in, only to see a plethora of mediocre paintings and statues scattered around, with apparently no rhyme or reason.

Next to a fake Picasso stood a medieval Madonna with golden halo, while poorly crafted knock-offs of paintings by Bouguereau stood next to Magrittes and Stellas.

Armand shook his head as he whispered to Andrea, "I love this guy's sense of organization, it reminds me of a Pollock—total chaos!"

Andrea chuckled as Pierre walked over to greet them. *"Bonjour. Puis je vous aider?"*

"Yes. Well, at least I hope you can help us," Andrea replied in French. "My husband and I are looking for something by Jean Carpeaux. Would you happen to have anything you can show us?"

"Ah, oui, suis moi," Pierre said matter-of-factly, as he turned around and walked away.

Armand snickered. "Geez! That's rude!"

Andrea giggled. "No, he said we should follow him."

Armand shrugged. "Oh, okay. I thought he gave us the famous French snub."

As they started to follow Pierre to the backroom, Armand looked around once more, and added with a whisper, "But, I suspect it's going to be a cheap replica, just like everything else here."

Andrea peered back over her shoulder and winked with a smile.

Yet as they entered the backroom, their faces wrinkled like prunes. The smell was downright nasty. Armand quickly located the culprit; a moldy Limburger sandwich sat amid a plate of escargot, which he surmised must have fled their shells to escape the horrid stench.

As they held their breath, Pierre picked up a statuette and walked toward them.

Armand was busy looking at the cheap trinkets in the storage room, when he turned and caught a glimpse of the finely crafted clay model. His eyes widened!

Meanwhile, Andrea leaned backward and discreetly spoke to Armand out of the corner of her mouth in English. "Like you said, just another fake. It's not even bronze or marble." Not hearing a response, she turned to notice Armand's enraptured stare. "What? You mean it's authentic?"

Armand nodded gently as he stepped in front of

Andrea and took hold of the statuette. His eyes scrutinized the two figures. He was well acquainted with the painting of *Pygmalion and Galatea* by Jean Gérôme, of the sculptor falling in love with his creation, and knew immediately that Carpeaux must have been in the process of making his own version based on Gérôme's masterpiece. Carpeaux and Gérôme were friends, and Carpeaux had even carved an elegant bust of Gérôme.

Furthermore, Armand knew how Carpeaux had mimicked his mentor, Francois Rude. He had made his own version of Rude's statue *Neapolitan Fisherboy*, utilizing almost the exact model with the same face and hat, yet he changed the posture and added a seashell in lieu of a turtle. Those alterations were enough to make his statue surpass his master's and become lauded by his peers and art critics. Now Armand could see the slight changes Carpeaux made to Gérôme's masterpiece. It didn't surpass his friend's work, at least not yet. But he new Carpeaux would rework his ideas, sometimes for years, as he did with his *Ugolino* masterpiece, just to obtain the precise configuration and emotional impact.

Meanwhile, the small clay statuette before them, although not a fully finished Carpeaux, was a valuable acquisition that any museum would relish in order to demonstrate the creation process of the master. But how it ended up in this man's chintzy shop of cheap trinkets and a chaotic array of fake canvases baffled Armand. His opinion about Pierre changed, believing him to be not a seasoned shyster but rather a poor judge of art, just struggling to make a buck.

He looked at Andrea. "Ask him how he came in possession of this piece."

Andrea did so, and Pierre replied, telling her that his aunt had left it to him in her will. But then Pierre asked why would Armand care, the statuette was only a cheap replica.

Armand looked back down at the statuette. He could tell Carpeaux's mastery of movement and had seen many of his clay busts. It undoubtedly was original. He looked at Andrea. "It's a good thing we came here before someone else ripped this poor man off. Please tell him he has an original Carpeaux, and it's worth twenty times more than the price tag he put on it."

As Andrea relayed the news, Pierre's face lit up. "*Oh mon Dieu. Merci! Merci!*"

Armand smiled. "I gather he said something about God and thanked us."

"Exactly," Andrea said.

Armand put the statuette down and pulled out his checkbook. "Ask him if he came across any other works by Carpeaux?"

Again Andrea translated the request as well as Pierre's response: "He said yes. In fact, he recently sold a clay bust by Carpeaux, which he now frets might also have been an original."

Armand stepped closer to Pierre and looked over at Andrea. "Ask him who was the bust of?"

Pierre offered a lengthy response, which Andrea translated: "He said the bust was of a nineteenth century composer, similar to the bust Carpeaux had done of Charles Gounod. However, this particular composer admired Dante and even wrote several piano pieces about the great poet and a tour de force of the Romantic era, the *Dante Symphony*."

Armand's eyes widened. "Franz Liszt!?" he exclaimed.

Oui, Monsieur, Franz Liszt..." Pierre said as he continued in French, which Andrea translated: "The Romantic era's ultimate pioneer. Yet, whose great name has not been lauded with the same verve and respect given to Bach, Mozart, or Beethoven, all of whom Liszt surpassed in the field of innovation, if not always in execution."

"Well said," Armand replied, knowing well how some of Liszt's compositions where mind-boggling and prophetic, yet were often like glittering gemstones placed in unpolished settings. Nevertheless, those precious gemstones influenced countless composers over numerous generations, while Liszt's incontestable masterpieces not only led and shaped his own Romantic era but also pioneered two new schools; namely Impressionism and Atonality. Those genres would flourish in the future, unfortunately with credit and praise bestowed upon others, specifically Debussy and Schoenberg respectively. Meanwhile, none of the greatest composers, whose names have been embedded in the minds of countless generations, could boast of such an achievement.

"So, tell me, do you have the name of the person who bought the Liszt bust?" Armand asked.

"I'm afraid not," Pierre replied in French, which Andrea translated. "I'm rather inept at keeping receipts. But more compelling still is the rumor that Carpeaux had finished drawing plans for an elaborate monument to Liszt, one that was supposed to adorn the entrance of the Liszt Academy in Budapest."

Armand's eyes oscillated in thought, as he said, "Dear Lord, that would be a fantastic find! Just imagine if Carpeaux's plans were used to fabricate the monument. It would be like the current plans to cast da Vinci's bronze horse from his sketches, giving life to the master's bold vision five centuries later."

Leonardo's ambitious plans for his colossal equestrian monument, if completed, would have dwarfed all others. Due to its monstrous size, the master had to develop new methods to cast and pour the bronze to ensure that the molten liquid would fill all parts of the cast before cooling. The brilliant artist/engineer not only solved all the technical problems he would encounter, but had even fashioned the huge, full-scale clay model of the horse, which amazed all who saw it, validating Leonardo as a true genius.

However, ominous clouds of war loomed on the horizon, and the bronze allotted for the monument went instead into fabricating cannons, turning Leonardo's luminous dream into a heartbreaking pile of rubble, as the dark side of human nature prevailed. On that fateful day, the pristine air was transformed into clouds of dust and death as French troops invaded Milan. In their wanton fury, they used Leonardo's clay horse for target practice, destroying what would have been a monumental achievement of unprecedented artistic and technological innovation.

As Armand contemplated the ill-fated failure to cast Leonardo's statue and now Carpeaux's *Liszt Monument*, he was deeply irritated, as the world had been robbed of two masterful works of art. Clearing his head, Armand looked up and thanked Pierre. He grasped his precious Carpeaux statuette, then turned eagerly toward Andrea and said, "Let's go!"

"Where to?" she asked, knowing when Armand was in super-sleuth mode.

"To Budapest."

"Budapest! *Hungary*?" she exclaimed.

"Yes, *I am...*" he said wittily, "but we can eat when we land in Budapest."

Four hours later, Armand and Andrea landed in Budapest. They rented a car and drove up Andrássy Avenue, arriving at the Liszt Academy of Music. The Academy was founded by the composer himself in 1875, and contains valuable manuscripts and books that were donated by the master upon his death.

As they walked up toward the huge edifice, built in the Neo-Renaissance style, Armand gazed up at the full-sized, sitting-statue of Liszt mounted on the third story of the building.

"Well, at least Hungary honors their hero properly," Armand said, as he spun around to look at the vast courtyard in front of the building. "And I can just imagine Carpeaux's glorious monument placed right here."

Andrea smiled at her idealistic husband. "Yes, it probably *would have* looked magnificent, honey. But don't get ahead of yourself. There's no way of knowing if Carpeaux's drawing even exists."

"Perhaps you're right," Armand said. "But one must always dream."

With that, the couple entered the building, where Sándor Nagy, President of the Academy, greeted them.

"Hello, Mr. and Mrs. Arnolfini," Sándor said in broken English. "Thank you for calling me in advance, as I have a busy schedule today. But I must say, I have read about some of your fascinating cases, so I'm intrigued, yet somewhat baffled." He pointed to a table in the lobby. "Please, have a seat."

As the threesome took their seats, he went on, "I imagine this is art related in some way, so, how could I possibly be of service?"

"I've recently been informed about an unknown drawing by Jean-Baptiste Carpeaux."

Sándor's eyebrows rose. "Ah, yes! You must be speaking of Carpeaux's monument to Liszt."

Armand leaned forward. "So, you've heard of this work?"

Sándor smiled. "Naturally. The drawing was in our very possession, and funding campaigns had even been implemented to initiate the great project. But, I'm afraid you wasted your time coming to Budapest, Mr. Arnolfini."

"Why is that?"

"Because Carpeaux's glorious plans disappeared in 1956, during the Hungarian Revolution. To refresh your memory, that's when my fellow Hungarians rose up to expel Soviet forces. And if you know your country's history, Mr.

Arnolfini, that is when America refused to help us break free of the communists' iron fist, shackles that still suppress us."

Armand shoulders wilted, as Andrea replied, "Mr. Nagy, Ronald Reagan was one of the few who spoke up back then to confront the communists, and although his advocacy wasn't embraced back then, as our president, he is determined to see his life-long mission come to fruition."

Sándor nodded as he raised his hands apologetically. "Yes, perhaps I shouldn't be so rash to blame your country, Mrs. Arnolfini. Every nation has an obligation to defend their own rights. But, even your Revolution to defeat the British was aided by the French. However, I'll agree; your current president *is* doing much to destabilize the Soviets. Freedom from tyranny looks closer than ever these days." He paused with a reflective smile, which quickly reverted back to his serious demeanor, as he looked at Armand. "But getting back to the lost Carpeaux drawing. The last person to literally see the plans was our former director, Tamás Kasza. He's currently eighty-nine years old and, I'm afraid, is in very bad health. So if you wish to speak to him, I'd suggest you do so quickly."

"We will. Thank you for your time," Armand said. "Can you tell us where Tamás lives?"

Sándor offered the address, and twenty minutes later, Armand and Andrea arrived at Tamás Kasza's house.

Knocking on the door, the couple was greeted by Christina, Kasza's nurse. After a brief round of introductions, Christina escorted them into Kasza's bedroom. Tamás was bedridden and hooked up to a series of monitors, with oxygen tubes up his nose, his skin pale with deathly shades of yellow and blue.

Christina adjusted the tubes and looked back at Armand. "He is very weak. So, please, don't ask him too many questions."

"No problem," Armand said. "I'll make it quick."

As Christina exited the bedroom, Armand stepped alongside the frail and dying old man. "Tamás," he said. "My name is Armand Arnolfini. I'm a private investigator. Sándor Nagy told me you have or had possession of Carpeaux's drawing of a *Liszt Monument*. Is that true, and if so, where is it?"

Tamás struggled to breathe as he looked up at the young and handsome private eye before him. His eyes veered over at Andrea, then back to Armand. "You make a fine looking couple. Enjoy your youth, it's fleeting."

Armand and Andrea smiled, as she said, "Thank you, Mr. Kasza, we will."

Meanwhile, Armand was acquainted with how old people could easily wander off on tangents, as he asked again, "The *Liszt Monument*, Tamás. What can you tell me about it?"

"Ah, yes," he said in a strained whisper. "It was quite beautiful, a splendid drawing. It would have been magnificent. But, unfortunately these damn communists trampled over our nation, both during and after the war. Animals! All of them!" he managed to muster with a cough.

Armand stepped closer and held his frail, wrinkled hand. "What did the Soviets do, Tamás?"

Kasza's glassy yellowed eyes veered up at Armand. "They stormed in and wreaked havoc. What else! I was well aware of how they looted great art, so I hid the drawing." Gasping for air, he choked, then regained his breath.

"Can I get you a drink of water?" Andrea said, as she stepped closer.

Tamás waved his bony hand. "No thank you, missy. But if you could prop me up a bit, that would be splendid."

As Andrea did so, Tamás's breathing improved slightly, as he looked back at Armand. "The main culprit was a Russian colonel, named Dima Ivanov, who later became a general."

"What about Ivanov?" Armand prodded.

Tamás's wrinkled face twisted, looking like a menacing gourd seen during Halloween, as he spat, "That bastard forced me under torture to reveal where I hid our valuable assets—the Carpeaux drawing among them." As Kasza's EKG monitor oscillated erratically and started to beep, he added, "And that was the last I saw of it."

Armand's shoulders sank. "And you have no idea where Dima took it?"

Christina reentered the room. "Please! You're getting Tamás agitated. I must ask you to leave!"

"Yes, of course," Armand said, while Tamás replied, "If you seek such answers, Mr. Arnolfini, I suggest you speak to Dima personally. The scoundrel is still alive."

As Armand and Andrea thanked Tamás and made for the door, Tamás added, "That's *if* you can get a straight answer from that vicious tyrant!"

Having left the house, Armand drove to the communist regime's headquarters, located in the magnificent Hungarian Parliament Building, and he parked the car. As Armand ran up the steps, Andrea tried to keep up.

Armand was furious; he loathed how militant brutes terrorized and suppressed nations, not to mention how they looted great cultural works of art. He stormed into the main office and asked the guard sitting at the front desk, "Where is Dima Ivanov? I wish to speak to him, *immediately*."

The guard looked at Armand, perplexed, while a bureaucrat in military uniform walked over. "Igor doesn't speak English. But if you're looking for General Ivanov, you're too late. He died two weeks ago."

Armand's temper wilted as he huffed. "Jesus Christ." He looked at the stone-faced bureaucrat. "Are you in charge here?"

"Yes, I'm Colonel Nikolai Valinski," he said with imperial gravity. "And who might you be?"

"I'm Armand Arnolfini," he said as he then pointed to Andrea. "And this is my wife, Andrea."

As all eyes in the office veered at the beautiful young lady before them, Armand continued, "I'm a private investigator, and I know General Ivanov confiscated a drawing by Jean Carpeaux, a French artist. Would any of you happen to know where it is? It was of a proposed monument dedicated to Franz Liszt. And I'd pay handsomely for it."

As the cadre of communist administrators cackled or sardonically snickered, a young bureaucrat, Adrian Minski, approached Andrea with an amorous smile and engaged her in conversation.

Meanwhile, Armand kept tabs on his wife out of the corner of his eye, as he pressed the Soviet snakes before him for an answer.

Colonel Valinski finally barked, "Mr. Arnolfini, we know of *no* such drawing. You've wasted your time and more importantly, *mine*! This matter is closed." He was about to turn and walk away, when he looked back at Armand and demanded, "Who told you this lie?"

Armand wasn't sure if these Soviet thugs would silence the person in question, so he replied vaguely: "It really doesn't matter, since he's on his deathbed." Armand grabbed Andrea's hand, and looked broadly over all of them. "I know one of you must know where it is. So, thanks, *for nothing!*" With that, he marched out the door, with Andrea in tow.

The couple hopped in their car, while a sea of irritated faces pressed up against the lobby's windows to watch the brazen P.I. drive off.

Armand's mind was clouded with failure. He couldn't believe he traveled all the way to Soviet-occupied Hungary to hit a dead end. All the leads, which at first appeared so promising, led to this belligerent Soviet block, one so dense and impenetrable that there was no way break through the communists' crypt of concealment. The hunt was over.

He looked at Andrea. "So, I saw that salacious slug slithering all around you. What did he want, other than squirming under your dress?"

Andrea chuckled, appreciating Armand's witty touch of jealousy. "Nothing of value, sweetheart, just another dead end. None of those Soviet goons could be trusted anyway."

"You've got that right," he said as he peered at the impressive Parliament building in his rearview mirror. "It makes me sick how those bastards took over this beautiful city, and this great nation."

"Well, their days are numbered, Armand. As I told Sándor, I truly believe Reagan's dealings with Gorbachev and his Star Wars initiative will end their reign."

"I hope so," Armand said as he pulled up to the exquisite Gundel restaurant and parked the car. He exhaled heavily, then looked at his lovely wife and said, "I think you'll enjoy this place. It's well over a hundred years old, and features some fine dishes."

Andrea blinked hard. "You've been here before?"

"Yes, when I was a *fútbol* player, living in Italy, I made a trip here to visit the Liszt Museum."

"Ah, yes, of course," Andrea said. "You have a thing for Liszt."

Armand smiled. "And rightfully so. Liszt was the Leonardo of music, multifaceted and a pioneer. Too bad the biased elites and ignorant critics still don't realize that."

Taking their seats in the opulent dining room, the couple gazed into each other's eyes, as the pangs of the world vanished amid a wellspring of tender love and affection. Engaging in diversionary conversation, they enjoyed a splendid dinner. Armand ate a succulent meal of *mangalitza* and quail, while Andrea ate tasty goulash, followed by dessert and coffee. All the while, a live gypsy band offered an evening of entertainment. Featured on their playlist were several Hungarian Rhapsodies by Liszt, which not only delighted Armand, but ended their Hungarian excursion with an authentic flare, one that helped sooth the sins of Soviet suppression.

Catching a flight, the couple arrived in LaGuardia Airport. They hailed a taxi, which drove them to their newly built home in Westport, Connecticut, which overlooked Long Island Sound. It was conveniently located halfway between Andrea's job in Hartford and Armand's Manhattan apartment, which he planned to convert to his office.

As they entered the house, Andrea dropped her suitcases and ran to the large windows in the rear den, which overlooked the Sound. Across the water, the faint vision of Long Island could be seen, as several sailboats peacefully cruised the waters. "Ah! This is spectacular, what a location!"

She spun around as Armand entered the room and walked up alongside her. He put his arm around her and drew her in close. Landing a loving kiss on her cheek, he said, "Yes, it's a great place to call home."

He looked around at the mostly vacant room. "It will be fun decorating this place. He raised both his hands and made a picture frame with his fingers. Pointing the frame at a vacant wall, he said, "I can envision a beautiful da Vinci here," shifting to another wall, he continued, "And perhaps a Caravaggio here," then shifting once again, he added, "And maybe even a vintage Barnum and Bailey poster right there."

Andrea laughed, as she hugged him tight. "Well, better a B&B poster than that ugly Feejee Mermaid you found!"

Armand chuckled. "Very true." He peered over at their empty new wall unit, and said with a smile, "And I can picture a hi-fi stereo right there, playing the romantic music of Liszt." His face mellowed. A smirk etched his handsome face, as his shoulders wilted. "Or perhaps Liszt's stormy or gloomy music," he said irritably. He walked over to the only chair in the room and sat down. Dejectedly he uttered, "I can't believe Carpeaux's drawing of the *Liszt Monument* is lost. I know those Soviet thugs know where it is."

Andrea walked over and sat on his lap. Compassionately, she brushed the hair away from his solemn eyes. "Well, even that sleazy bureaucrat, Adrian Minski, who tried to hit on me, said it's lost." As Armand barely heard her, lost in thought, she added, "He said a Russian aristocrat had it, but he, too, died. So there's no way we'll ever find out where it is, that's *if* it still even exists."

Armand's ears perked up, as he leaned forward and looked deep into her eyes. "Hold on! A Russian aristocrat had possession of it?"

91

Andrea squirmed in his lap, sensing Armand's rising curiosity, as she said innocently, "Well, yes, Adrian said a nobleman, named Valdoff, bought it from General Ivanov."

Armand's body jolted as he grabbed Andrea's waist and lifted her off his lap. "Valdoff!?" he blurted. "*Boris* Valdoff?"

"Yes, I believe so, why?" She said, now standing before him and looking down into his electrified eyes. "You know him?"

"Know him!?" Armand exclaimed as he sprang to his feet. "I wrestled that drunken Cossack to the floor, he hit his head, blacked out, and was dragged away by Interpol. *Yes*, I know him! Why didn't you mention this earlier?"

"Well, he's dead now," Andrea said. "So, it's just another dead end, literally."

"I think not," Armand said as he scrambled for the phone. "Last I heard, Boris was in prison from my Russian Link case. Perhaps Adrian only cared to offer you half the story to get us off the trail, or to protect his ass." He lifted the phone and started punching in numbers. "I need to call Louis Gaspard at Interpol to see if Valdoff is still alive and in prison in Stuttgart, Germany."

As Louis answered, Armand made the query, to which Gaspard replied, "Yes, Armand, Valdoff *is* alive. But I have bad news; he's due to be released today, in two hours."

"Shoot!" Armand huffed. "Wait! Agent Otto Krüger is still stationed in Stuttgart, isn't he?"

"I believe so, why?"

"I can't make it there in two hours, but Otto can. Please call him. Tell him to tail Boris until I arrive. I don't want to lose sight of this creep."

"You got it!" Louis said, and quickly hung up.

Armand looked at Andrea. "Well, I guess you know what this means. I'm heading to Germany."

Andrea nodded solemnly. "I was hoping to spend some down-time with you, Armand. We've been running around ever since we visited Ghent and got married."

"Yes, I know, sweetheart, but as I had told you, when a trail is hot, you have to take it, before it turns cold." He hugged her tight and kissed her on the cheek. "I'll only be gone for a week or so. When I return, we'll spend quiet-time around here..." he looked at the empty walls, and added, "and have fun decorating this place together."

She kissed him on the lips. "Well, at least you're already packed."

With a chuckle, Armand spun around and headed toward the door.

Several hours later, Armand landed in Stuttgart, Germany, and was greeted by Agent Otto Krüger. Armand's eyes widened. "What are you doing *here*, Otto!? You didn't lose him, did you?"

Otto laughed. *"Nein, mein Freund!* Chill that hot Italian blood. Everything is under control." As the two walked toward Otto's car, he continued, "Boris was greeted by two, known Russian racketeers upon his release. They drove him to his villa, not far from here." He opened the passenger door. "Hop in, I'll take you there."

Dashing through the streets, Otto and Armand finally arrived at Valdoff's sprawling villa. Conveniently nestled in a wooded cove, the villa sat hidden behind two large stone pillars with a decorative wrought iron gate. Mounted on one of the pillars was a large plaque, with the initials "BV" in gold letters.

As the car's wheels rolled over the cobbled-stoned driveway, they saw Boris putting briefcases in the trunk of his metallic-gold Rolls Royce.

Otto stopped the car, as Armand jumped out and marched toward Valdoff.

Boris heard the footsteps and spun around. His eyes bulged! "Albrecht Schumann!" he growled. "*Ty negodyay!* (You rascal!)," he spat in Russian, then continued in English in his thick accent, "I spent five years in prison because of you!"

Otto came up alongside Armand and looked at his partner, who discreetly winked, reminding Krüger of his undercover name, as Armand responded, "And are you looking to spend another five years in a cell, Boris?"

"*Dlya chego?*" he blustered in Russian, then corrected himself in English, "For what?"

"What's in those briefcases?" Armand demanded, as he walked toward the trunk of the Rolls Royce.

"None of your damned business!"

Armand reached in and snapped open one of the cases, as Boris grabbed his wrist. "*Stoy!* (Halt!) You have no right going through my luggage!"

Armand's eyes widened as he picked up an original woodcut print by Albrecht Dürer. "Ah! *The Lamentation* by Dürer. How nice." He looked up at Boris. "But, it appears you'll be the one lamenting, Boris, when we throw your fat ass back in prison."

Boris's eyes veered over Armand's shoulder. "I think not!"

Just then, Armand fell to his knees as he dropped the woodcut and held his throbbing head. Boris caught the precious artifact before it hit the ground, but the two ruffians behind Armand responded quickly: one stout goon grabbed Armand by the hair and pulled him up, while the taller, pock-faced thug drew out his Glock and fired at Otto, who had already pulled out his gun.

Unfortunately, Otto was two seconds too late, as the thug's bullet shattered his clavicle before exiting out of his back. Otto dropped the gun and held his wound as the thug fired another shot, straight through Otto's forehead. Otto fell fatally backward as Armand elbowed the stocky goon behind him, who gasped for air.

Armand grabbed the briefcase and flung it at the gun-wielding thug's hand. As the Glock fell to the ground, Armand dashed to retrieve it. The thug jumped on his back, and the two wrestled on the cobblestoned pavement.

Meanwhile, Boris picked up the briefcase and hopped in the Rolls. As he fumbled to find his keys, Armand had already subdued the killer, slipped the Glock in his back pocket, and then finished off the stout goon with a solid soccer kick to the gut and a crack to the head.

As the Rolls Royce started to move, Armand turned and ran alongside the car, grabbing the driver's side door handle. Boris tried to lock the door, but wasn't quick enough, as Armand opened the door and belted Boris in the face. Boris spit blood, then wrestled with the door, trying to close it, but Armand's superior strength prevailed. He swung open the door, grabbed Boris by the collar, and dragged him out, while the shiny metallic Rolls continued forward, crashing into the stone pillar of the entry gate with a loud thud.

Steam belched out of the mangled grill and buckled hood, while Armand pulled the Glock out of his back pocket and bellowed, "You SOB! Now look what you've done!" Armand glanced back at Otto's languid carcass, then back at Boris. "If you would have cooperated, Boris, we might have even let you off with a slap on the wrist, *if* you would have just told us where Carpeaux's drawing is. But now you and your gangster buddies will stand trial." Gazing back at the pock-faced killer, Armand spat through his teeth, "And *that* bastard will be charged with murder!"

Just then, the thug rose to his feet and pulled out another gun, hidden in his sock. As he aimed at Armand, a bullet already left Armand's chamber and bore a hole in the killer's pocked-face, adding another crater, this one far larger and bloody, as the thug fell backward and hit the pavement.

"Correction," Armand said. "*That* bastard can now be embalmed."

He looked back at Boris and stuck the still-hot nozzle of the Glock in his fleshy cheek. Boris yelped, as Armand growled, "Now tell me, where the hell did you hide the Carpeaux drawing? And don't piss me off, Boris. Because if you lie, I *will* blow your head off!"

Boris's nerves rattled as sweat poured out of his massive head. "*Khorosho*! (Okay!)" he pleaded. "Relax!"

"How the hell can I relax, you moron!?" Armand spat. "My buddy is *dead*, and you once again have me involved in your dirty smuggling ring." He pressed the gun deeper into Boris' face. "You have two options, meathead. You can speak to *me*..." He pulled back the trigger. "Or to Lucifer! Which is it?"

"*Khorosho!*" Valdoff stammered. "It's s-still in the h-house. I'll get it for you."

"You better not be lying, Boris! Or this bullet will bore through your fat head!"

"No! No! I'm *not*," he pleaded. "You prevented me from packing the car. *Klyanus'* (I swear). Let me up. I'll show you."

Armand backed off, as Boris rose to his feet. They walked past the two corpses and the unconscious goon and entered the villa. Boris led the way, as he walked through the marble-floored foyer, and then entered the library. The spacious room was lined with mahogany bookshelves and wainscot panels, each nine feet high. Boris slid open one of the wooden panels, revealing a secret passageway. The two walked down a flight of narrow stairs and came upon a cellar. Several empty picture frames were stacked neatly against a wall, while nearby was a table with the Carpeaux drawing spread out, sitting amid the dim glow of a fluorescent light above.

"There, I told you," Boris said in his raspy Russian voice. "It is in fine condition."

As Armand approached the drawing, his eyes widened with awe—the design was utterly spectacular. He scanned the *Liszt Monument*, from its unique base, featuring a grand piano, flanked by violins, cellos, woodwinds, and brass instruments, then upward, to see a group of three sculpted full-sized portraits of the composer: One of Liszt as a child prodigy, another in mid-age, wearing a crown, having been honored as the unrivalled King of the Piano, and one in old age, sitting solemnly in his abbé's cassock, scribbling out the enigmatic innovations that would inspire future generations and engender two new genres.

Armand was deeply moved; Carpeaux had beautifully captured Liszt's prophetic symphonic poem, *From the Cradle to the Grave*, which was structured in a similar triad arrangement, of youth, middle age, and old age.

Armand shook his head in wonder. "This is truly magnificent!" He turned to share his excitement with Boris, but saw a horrific sight instead, as Boris doused the drawing with a can of fluid!

Armand tried to grab the can, but a drop of liquid scorched his hand. Gazing down at the drawing, it soon became clear; Boris had thrown sulfuric acid on Carpeaux's masterpiece. Armand stood in shock, and helpless, as the precious drawing shriveled up before his eyes, while noxious fumes drifted upward, stinging his nostrils and burning his eyes.

Armand covered his nose and pointed the Glock at Boris. "What the hell is wrong with you!? How could you ruin a priceless work of art?"

Boris's thick meaty lips twisted with animus. "If I'm to go back to jail, *no one* will have the pleasure of seeing it."

Armand shook his head in disbelief. "You're supposed to be an art connoisseur, Boris. How could you do such a thing?"

"*Ochen' prosto* (Very simple)," he said with a warped smile. "Actually, I'm glad you got to see it with your own eyes," he said maliciously. "Now you know how something very precious can be lost, *like my freedom!*"

Armand huffed and retorted, "You forfeited your freedom by being a hoodlum, Boris. And there's nothing precious about a two-bit thief." He glanced back at the smoldering artifact. "Yet, you destroyed a precious work of art by Carpeaux, one that could have been used to erect a bronze or marble statute to a great man, perhaps the music world's most innovative composer of all time." Armand's lips furled with anger. "How dare you! You selfish imp!"

Boris just looked at Armand with a proud and indignant stare, then said, "Yes, I love art. But I am of royal blood. And I am just as precious as any great work of art."

Armand almost gagged. "Yes, and like a great work of art, locked in a museum for safekeeping, you, too, will be locked away for safekeeping, Boris. Except, no one will come to visit you in your confined gallery. Now move!" he growled as he waved the gun toward the exit.

Boris rolled his eyes and wobbled slowly back up the stairs, mumbling under his breath. As Boris reached the library, he swiftly closed the secret panel behind him on Armand's face, then dashed toward the door. Armand slid open the panel and chased after him. Boris ran out the front entrance and onto the driveway, while Armand finally reached the front door, but instead came face-to-face with the barrel of a gun.

The stout goon had recovered the gun, which he now pointed at Armand's head. "Enough of the games!" he barked in his Russian accent. "Put the gun down, unless you want to join your dead comrade!"

Meanwhile, Boris ran into his four-car garage and started his Mercedes. Armand lowered his gun and motioned with his head toward Boris. "You can stand here making threats, gorilla head, but your boss is leaving you behind, *chump*!"

As the goon turned, Armand's Glock came crashing across his face. The thug staggered backward while Armand quickly grabbed the goon's gun and pummeled him hard in the solar plexus. This time, the hoodlum lost his breath and fell backward, while both guns were now in Armand's possession.

Armand leapt over him and raced toward the garage door. Just then, the Mercedes sped out, almost knocking Armand to the ground, as Boris raced down the driveway. Armand spun around and pointed his Glock at the rear tire of the Mercedes. He pulled the trigger and blew out the left rear tire, causing the car to spin out of control. The Mercedes crashed into the mangled Rolls Royce with a loud thunderclap of metal and broken glass. Armand ran up to the vehicle and pointed the gun at Boris' head. "Get out! *Now!*"

Boris snorted as he wiped the blood away from his swollen nose and bloody lips. Irritably, he wriggled his way out of the car, just as an Interpol van drove up and stopped before them. Two agents hopped out, as one said, "Otto radioed us. But I see you have everything under control."

Armand's shoulders wilted as he glanced back toward the two bodies lying on the pavement, each corpse sitting in their own languid pool of blood. "Well, certainly not everything."

The other agent dashed toward Otto Krüger's body. Tears welled in his eyes, as he glanced back at his partner. "Aw, s-shit!" he said as his voice cracked. "Otto's dead, Rolf." He gritted his teeth. "We're too late!"

Rolf's eyes pinched closed. "*Gottverdammt!*" he cussed in German. He reopened his eyes, which quickly zeroed in on Boris, then darted over at Armand. "Did that fat pig kill him? Huh? Tell me!" he seethed through gritted teeth.

Armand sighed. "No. He's just a repulsive vandal and a thief. He destroyed a precious work of art by Jean Carpeaux." He looked back at the dead, hit man on the ground. "*That's* the pig who killed Otto."

Four hours later, Interpol finished debriefing Armand at headquarters and had Boris firmly locked up.

Rolf looked at Armand. "Don't worry, Arnolfini, this time Valdoff won't get released."

Armand looked at Boris, who just crossed his arms and snickered.

"Good," Armand said. "As Boris told me, he's just as great as any great work of art." Armand turned, and as he walked away, he added, "Just make sure he stays in your permanent collection."

THE POE-POURRI MYSTERY

Having retuned home from Germany—after the ill-fated Carpeaux Caper ended with the death of Otto Krüger and the destruction of Carpeaux's *Liszt Monument* drawing— Armand spent the last two weeks at home trying to forget the tragic losses by fixating on three things; namely, the incarceration of Boris Valdoff, the acquisition of the Carpeaux statuette, and spending time with Andrea decorating their newly built home in Westport, Connecticut.

Armand plopped on their new Ralph Lauren sofa in the den after several hours of installing furniture and, more importantly, hooking up his Pioneer SX-1010 receiver to a pair of Pioneer CS-99 speakers, which played the title track from the Moody Blues latest album, *The Other Side of Life*.

Meanwhile, Andrea was filling up a stylish glass bowl with potpourri, happy to have convinced Armand to decorate the den in a decidedly American fashion, in lieu of his favorite Italian Renaissance style. Armand had conceded to utilizing the Italianate décor to flush out his home office and elaborate library, which sat in the west wing of their 5,000 square-foot home, so he was now quite content; having pleased his wife and listening to a splendid piece of music.

Just then, the phone rang and Andrea picked up the receiver. Meanwhile, Armand thumbed through the case of CDs beside him on the sofa, as the names of Pink Floyd, Yes, Renaissance, and Blue Oyster Cult flipped by. On to the classical section, the names of Shostakovich, Tchaikovsky, Sibelius, Liszt and Penderecki flashed by, when his finger skipped back to the progressive section and stopped on *Tales of Mystery and Imagination* by the Alan Parsons Project.

As he opened the CD case and pulled out the disc, Andrea hung up and said, "Don't bother putting that on."

"Why? You don't like Alan Parsons?"

Andrea chuckled. "I don't even know what CD you have in your hand, honey. I'm referring to another investigation that needs your attention."

Armand's shoulders sank. "Geez, I was hoping to chill out. What gives?"

Andrea stepped closer as she straightened out the Tommy Hilfiger throw pillows on the sofa and solemnly sat down beside him. "My friend, Martha Harrington, works at the Edgar Allan Poe Cottage Museum in the Bronx." She swallowed hard. "She said there's been a brutal, and very mysterious, double murder at the museum. The police are baffled and have no suspects, especially since the two dead victims appeared to be the criminals."

Armand glanced at the CD that was eerily in his hand and put it down. The coincidence of Alan Parson's album dedicated to Poe was almost as hard to process as this baffling murder mystery now presented to him. He looked at Andrea and held her hand. "That's awful." He blinked hard. "Wait a minute! You just said another investigation that needs *my* attention. I don't handle homicide cases, sweetheart. You know that."

"Yes, but let's face it, Armand, you've been on plenty of cases that involved murder, just like your last two." She glanced at his shirt. "You even have a bullet wound in your chest to prove it."

Armand shook his head with a stifled chuckle. "Sweetheart, that's collateral damage. I hunt down art thieves and forgers."

"Yes, and some have been murderers, from Russian gangsters to coldblooded Nazi psychopaths."

Armand nodded with a smile. "Yes, you're right at that."

"Good!" She said. "Then it's settled. Let's get going, I told Martha we'll be there in forty-five minutes."

Andrea got up, fetched her coat, and looked back at Armand. "Well? Come on!"

Armand shook his head and sighed. "Okay. But I'm only going to take a cursory look, that's all."

"Yes, yes, of course," Andrea said, knowing well that once Armand gets a first-hand look at the evidence, he'll change his insatiably curious mind.

Forty-seven minutes later, the couple arrived at the Edgar Allan Poe Cottage in their 1937 Cord Coupe. The small white farmhouse had been moved from its original location in

Fordham to its present location near the Grand Concourse in the Bronx.

In 1894, Louis Aloys Risse, a French immigrant, had modeled the Grand Concourse upon the Champs-Élysées in Paris, but on a larger scale. Once a prestigious section of the Bronx, the area experienced an exodus of its wealthy residents during the sixties, giving way to crime, thus despoiling what had once been a golden gem of a brighter time.

As Armand and Andrea walked up to the small cottage, Martha came out and escorted them inside. Turning around, she said with a quiver, "It's terrible, just terrible! The thought of such a ghastly double murder, right here, where I've worked for many years, scares the dickens out of me."

Armand looked around and was a bit baffled, as he inquired, "Where are the police? Or the tape barriers to ward off the crime scene?"

Martha swallowed hard. "Well, truth be told, this crime occurred three and a half weeks ago. You see, it's been decided that it would be best to keep a low profile." She glanced at the only two visitors who just exited. "This museum struggles to make ends meet, and well, we don't wish to scare away business. Bad press we don't need."

"No wonder I never heard anything about it on the news," Andrea said.

Armand rubbed his chin. "So, why did you call us? Aren't the police working this case?"

"No, not really," Martha said. "They haven't made much progress, and have only one officer following up leads, *if* they arise. So, I fear the culprit will never be found. I work here, sometimes alone. So, plainly put, I'm scared. This isn't located in the best of neighborhoods."

Andrea looked at Armand. "You have to help her, Armand. You know how the police can drag their feet or even abandon cases."

Armand didn't wish to step further into this case, but his curiosity was also tugging at his brain. He looked at Martha. "Well, at least give me the rundown. Where were the two bodies found?"

Martha pointed out the window. "One was found just outside this window, on the lawn, with his throat cut. Police identified him as Jamal Johnson."

"I see the window panes and sash have been repaired," Armand said. "I'm guessing he was thrown out the window?"

"Yes!" Martha said surprised. "You really *are* quite observant." She looked at Andrea. "You were right, I'm already impressed."

"He's the best," Andrea replied proudly.

Armand sighed. "Listen, let's not get too excited over one little observation. Besides, I'm here only as an observer. I can't commit to anything, just yet. Now, please proceed; where was the other body found?"

Martha's grin morphed into a pout. She glanced at Andrea; she expected that Armand had already accepted the case. She then turned and pointed to the fireplace. "That's an even more bizarre murder," she said. "The body of Tyron Daniels was found severely bludgeoned and stuffed up the chimney."

Andrea almost choked. "Up the chimney!?"

Martha looked at her. "Yes. And he was found with Edgar Allan Poe's precious pen in his pocket. The very pen, we believe, that Poe used to write *The Raven*, as well as other famous poems and short stories."

Armand's curiosity was mushrooming, as he said, "Precious pen indeed! I imagine that artifact is worth quite a bit."

Martha nodded. "Oh, yes. It's our prized possession."

Armand walked over to the fireplace and peered up the chimney. It was narrow and sooty, a tight fit for a human body, one that could surely suspend a corpse, at least for a period of time. He gazed down to see that the brick floor of the firebox was stained with crimson hues of blood. He looked back at Martha. "I'd suggest using muriatic acid to clean the blood off these bricks, Martha, otherwise some visitors might get curious, or even alarmed."

"Yes, I've been putting it off," Martha said. "It's kind of creepy, you know, to clean up a dead person's blood." She squinted. "But, muriatic acid, you say." She grasped a pad and pencil and jotted it down. "I'll have to pick up some tomorrow morning. Thank you."

"So, nothing else was taken? Just the pen?"

Martha looked out the window. "Well, *that* thief tried to get away with an authentic first edition of Poe's famous poem, *Annabel Lee*, which Poe had made notations in. It's also quite valuable." She turned, glanced at the bedroom door, then back at Armand. "If you're not familiar with that poem, it's about a man's love for a beautiful woman. His love was so great and sublime that even the angels were envious. It was a profound love, one that the narrator in the poem retained, even after Annabel died." A tear welled in Martha's eye.

Andrea reached over and grasped her friend's hand.

"Yes, that *is* beautiful," Andrea said, knowing that Martha's husband, and love of her life, had died a year prior. "I know how much you miss William."

Martha nodded solemnly. "Yes, I do. And, in a small way, it mirrors Edgar's inspiration for that beautiful poem." She peered back at the bedroom door. "That's the room and bed Edgar's wife Virginia had died in. She was only twenty four years old."

The room fell silent, until Armand uttered, "Dear God. That *is* terrible. I wasn't aware of that."

"Yes," Martha said. "Virginia was half his age, and his first cousin. But he loved her beyond the bounds of this world, as his words continue to echo down the corridors of time, for all time."

Armand swallowed hard as his emotions took hold of him. He gazed at Andrea, dreading the mere thought of losing her. Andrea caught his doleful, loving stare and smiled, silently conveying that her heart beat in unison with his.

Armand broke his morose trance and looked back at Martha. "I'll do my best to find out what really happened here, Martha. Since those valuable items were not stolen, it appears some vigilante caught these thieves red-handed and took matters into his or her own hands. Or perhaps it was a hit by a rival gang, if these thieves had criminal records or if it was drug related. But I can tell you one thing for sure, this crime was *not* committed by an orangutan."

Martha and Andrea squinted, as Andrea said, half-embarrassed, "*Orangutan*!? How can you joke at a time like this?"

"I'm not," Armand said, as his eyes scanned both their faces. "Evidently, you both failed to see the connection. These murders just so happen to mimic Poe's seminal work, *The Murders in the Rue Morgue*."

Martha's eyes rolled in thought for a moment, as the visions of Poe's tale melded with the reality before them. "Ah! Yes, of course," she said. "I haven't read that story in years, but how could I have missed that?"

Andrea was still confused. "Missed what? Tell me?"

Martha looked at her friend. "In Poe's tale, an orangutan had escaped its owner and killed two people in the same fashion. But those victims were both women. I suppose that's what also threw me off."

"Yes," Armand said. "And one was stuffed up a chimney. Auguste Dupin, Poe's famous detective, surmised that the strength needed to achieve such a feat had to be by someone with superhuman strength, or an animal. In that case, an orangutan."

Andrea was equally surprised by Armand's literary knowledge. "*You've* read Poe?"

Armand nodded. "Yes. Well, not all of his works. But what most people don't realize is that Poe invented the detective story. And *The Murders in the Rue Morgue* was the first story in history to feature a detective using logic and analysis, as well as forensics. It became the template for all others that followed. Doyle's Sherlock Holmes and Agatha Christie's Hercule Poirot are indebted to Poe's Auguste Dupin, not to mention how Alfred Hitchcock attributed his career to Poe's suspenseful tales."

Andrea smiled. It now made sense. How could her clever sleuth of a husband not be interested in Poe?

Meanwhile, Armand looked back at Martha. "Can you tell me the name of the officer handling this case? I'd like to speak with him."

Martha grinned. "Does this mean you're taking on the case?"

"That's a yes, Martha. How could I neglect to defend Poe's legacy?"

"Thank you!" she said excitedly. "It's officer Kevin O'Reilly of the 64th Precinct." Unexpectedly, her smile vanished. "Uh, but hold on. This little museum doesn't have enough money to pay someone like *you*."

"Don't worry," Armand said. "We'll work something out later." He looked around the small cottage. "Do you mind if I take a look around?"

"No, by all means," she said.

Armand strolled around, scrutinizing the premises, while Martha and Andrea sat at the dining room table and caught up on personal matters.

On the wall, the clock ticked, as the sun cast its fading rays upon the west facade of the building and the sky darkened. Reentering the cottage museum, Armand rejoined the two ladies. "I didn't find a thing," he said, disappointed. "The place is clean as a whistle. Yet, after almost a month, I imagine it would be." He looked at Martha. "Have you noticed anyone suspicious before the crime?"

Martha stood up and nodded. "Yes, the police already questioned him three weeks ago. His name is Eddie Landau. He's a bit of an odd ball. Before being questioned, he visited the museum quite regularly, and is...well, *odd*. A bit obsessed with Poe."

"You mean like someone who would kill to protect his idol?" Armand surmised.

Again, Martha nodded. "Yes, I believe so. But the police said he's clean."

"Well, I guess it's time I pay officer O'Reilly a visit." Armand looked at his watch. "It's getting late, but I *will* see him tomorrow, first thing."

As Andrea stood up, Martha gazed at the clock. "Dear me, I need to close up. Well, thank you for taking on this case, Armand."

"My pleasure," he said. "I'll get back to you once I get more information. Good night."

With that, Andrea and Martha said their good-byes, then the Arnolfinis walked to their '37 yellow Cord and headed home.

The next morning, Armand arrived at the 64th Precinct in the Bronx. He went inside and located officer Kevin O'Reilly, who was lanky with red hair and freckles. Armand sat in the metal chair beside his desk, which was surrounded by a labyrinth of other desks amid aisles that appeared like busy streets, as officers scurried to and fro like police cars in pursuit.

Armand glanced around, sensing that chaos was the order of the day at the 64th Precinct, as arresting officers walked in with handcuffed criminals, while others typed away their arrest reports. He turned his attention to officer O'Reilly, who finally looked up at Armand. "So, you said on the phone you're investigating the Poe Cottage murders. How can I help you?"

Armand drew his chair closer. "Martha Harrington told me you questioned a suspect, named Eddie Landau. Why didn't he fit the profile?"

"Have you ever met Eddie?"

"No, but Martha says he's odd, or rather *obsessed* with Poe. And he's large and strong enough to commit those two extremely brutal and unusual murders."

O'Reilly took a sip of his Coca Cola, then said, "Yes, but Eddie wouldn't have the brains or guts to do something so vicious and horrific like that. He's large, yes. But more like Baby Huey than Baby Face Nelson, if you get my drift."

Armand leaned back. "Yes, but psychological abnormalities, like schizophrenia, bipolar disorder, or multiple personality disorder, can yield unexpected results."

O'Reilly rolled his eyes. "I'm not paid to be a psychiatrist or psychologist or whatever, Mr. Arnolfini. So, I'm not about to speculate on a spectrum of disorders. Hard evidence is what I need, and Eddie didn't indicate anything worthy of my time. I even had him tailed for two weeks, yet nothing abnormal appeared, other than his visiting the museum four times, which he then stopped doing. Perhaps he spotted my undercover guy, but in any case, I dropped him as a suspect. More importantly, just this morning, my captain told us to drop the case. As you can see, we have tons of other cases to handle."

Just then, an officer bumped into Armand's chair while dashing to the fax machine.

O'Reilly picked up several papers on his desk and started to peruse them, as he said with disinterest, "So, if there's nothing else, I have work to do."

"Yes, there *is* something else," Armand said louder, making sure officer O'Reilly was paying attention. "I would like to know why a *double murder* is being dropped?"

O'Reilly slammed the papers down, and looked up into Armand's eyes. "Look around, Mr. Arnolfini! This place is a madhouse. We have shootings, rapes, and DOAs every day here. It's the Bronx." He huffed and shook his head, then added, "Besides, nothing was even stolen from the museum, everything was found on the dead bodies. It's a clean, open and shut, case."

"Clean!?" Armand jabbed. "Two bloody bodies were found, one with a sliced throat and tossed out a window, and the other bludgeoned, mangled, and stuffed up a chimney! The only thing clean about this case was the crime scene. I couldn't find a single clue."

As other officers turned and listened to Armand's rousing conversation, O'Reilly irritably tried to end their meeting, as he said, "Well, you're not alone, I got to the scene the very next morning, but didn't find a thing, either." He paused, then added, "Except for the chief's 'Captain Badge', which fell off, and I gave it back to him. So, there are no clues to go on. Case closed."

Just then, officer Juarez, at the adjacent desk, got up and took three steps over. "Actually, I was the first one at the scene," he said looking down at Armand. "I'm officer Omar Juarez, the videographer. I film crime scenes before anyone disturbs them, then shoot plenty of footage afterwards to document everything." His eyes veered back toward his desk. "I have it right here, if you're interested?"

"Certainly! Thank you," Armand said, as he stood up and stepped over, while O'Reilly rolled his eyes.

As Juarez played back the video, Armand looked on intently, with all senses in-tune.

On the screen, a vision of the Poe Cottage came into view as Juarez walked toward the structure, then around the perimeter of the building. Coming into view was the dead body of Jamal Johnson on the lawn. The camera zoomed in on the body, capturing the deceased in all different angles, with special attention to the victim's slit throat and his bloodstained shirt. The camera then panned over to capture the arrival of officers O'Reilly, three others, and the coroner. In the background, an ambulance and EMT workers stood idly by, drinking coffee and waiting for orders.

The three officers closed off the perimeter of the Poe Cottage with red barricade tape, while the coroner inspected the bodies. Officer O'Reilly was several yards back, speaking to Martha Harrington. However, their conversation was inaudible. The camera then panned to capture Captain McDoogal as he arrived. With a slight stagger, McDoogal made his way hurriedly to the crime scene, coming into full view of the camera lens. He asked Juarez, "Has any evidence been found?"

Officer Juarez's voice sounded in response: "Not that I'm aware of, Captain. Whoever killed them left this place clean."

A voice off screen was then heard: "Nothing yet, Captain, except your badge." Just then, officer O'Reilly appeared on screen and handed Captain McDoogal his badge.

"Thank you," McDoogal said, while O'Reilly looked at the camera, shook his head discreetly, then looked back at the Captain, and said, "Martha Harrington, the curator, said there's been a strange character visiting the museum fairly often. He goes by the name of Eddie Landau. She suggests we question him."

"Excellent!" McDoogal said as he pinned his badge back on. "We have a s-suspect already. Good w-work, Kevin!" he added with a slight slur.

Again, O'Reilly looked at the camera, this time running his finger across his neck.

The camera cut out, then quickly panned back to the dead body on the lawn.

At that point, Armand said, "Hold on! Stop the video."

Omar paused the video. "I know what you're going to ask. Why did officer O'Reilly ask me to cut filming? Right?"

Officer O'Reilly interjected, "You shouldn't even be showing him that video, Omar!"

Armand glanced at O'Reilly, then looked back at Omar. "I surmised why you panned away, officer Juarez. It's clear that the Captain was drunk or hung-over."

"Yeah, he was at a police gala the night before," Juarez admitted.

"Well, I don't care much about that," Armand said. "What I do care about is his badge."

"What about the badge?" Officer O'Reilly interjected again. "I told you I found it on the ground and gave it back to him. Didn't you just see that!?" he snapped.

Armand looked at O'Reilly. "Yes, I saw that. But, apparently, you all overlooked a critical aspect of that transaction."

"Yeah? And what's that?" O'Reilly said cockily.

"The Captain arrived at the scene *without* his badge," Armand said. "Therefore, he didn't lose it while he was there that morning. Evidently, he was at the crime scene before any of you arrived."

O'Reilly squinted, retracing the steps, while officer Juarez said, "Damn! You're right, Mr. Arnolfini." He scratched his goatee in thought, then added, "Come to think of it, that was the Captain's day off. He had told me he planned to be out that day, so he could recoup after the gala. Yet…" Suspiciously, he looked back at the video screen. "He came to the crime scene instead."

"Exactly," Armand said.

"So, why was he there?" Juarez said in a nervous whisper.

As O'Reilly gritted his teeth, Armand said, "I assume to get his badge before any of you found it, or put two and two together."

"Well, clearly we didn't add much of anything together," Juarez said. "At least not until *you* showed up."

O'Reilly's face stiffened as he barked, "That doesn't mean a damn thing! I'm not following you two clowns down this dirty road you're heading. So, I'd advise you both to shut up!"

Armand looked over at O'Reilly. "Shut up? You mean like how Captain McDoogal *shut up* about being at the crime scene before any of you, or how he *shut down* this case?"

"You're making wild and unsubstantiated accusations, Mr. Arnolfini!"

"The only thing wild, officer O'Reilly, is apparently your Captain. First, he shows up at the crime scene to retrieve his badge, one he lost there before the crime was even reported. Second, he fails to mention that he was at the scene previously. Third, he has you waste time questioning and following Eddie Landau. And lastly, he shuts this double murder case down after less than a month."

Juarez chimed in, "And come to think of it, he's the one who ordered us to keep the media out of this."

Armand's eyes widened. *"He* ordered the media blackout? I thought Martha Harrington did?"

Before officer O'Reilly could fire back, Captain Jack McDoogal replied, "You have something to say to me, Mr. Arnolfini?" as he stepped out of his office and into the mounting dissonance.

Armand looked up at the tall, stone-faced captain. "Yes, in fact, I do,"

"Then let's take it in my office," he said firmly, as he gave officer Juarez a deadly stare. With that, McDoogal stood militantly erect, with an intensity akin to General Patton, as Armand walked past him and entered his office. The six-foot-four mountain of a man then marched in behind him and shut the door.

McDoogal took his seat behind his desk, towering over it like a gorilla hovering over a crate of bananas, waiting to defend them from the irritating intruder before him, as he said, "I overheard some of your conversation, Mr. Arnolfini. You're a private eye, and a ballsy one at that."

"Yes, I am, Captain, on both accounts," Armand said as he sat in the chair before him. "But the latter account is only when situations warrant it."

The Captain snickered, amused. "And I suppose *I* warrant it?"

"Yes, I believe you do, Captain. There are certainly many questions that need to be answered."

"I have nothing to hide, Mr. Arnolfini. Fire away," the Captain said confidently, as he leaned back.

"Very well," Armand said. "I'm curious to hear your explanations regarding the series of suspicious actions you've taken. First off, you visited the crime scene on your day off, then ordered a media blackout. You're obviously a big and strong man, one who could easily carry out this brutal crime, and we have evidence of you on film, not wearing the badge when you arrived, and the badge being found *at* the crime scene. That's hard evidence, Captain, that you were at the scene *before* the crime was even reported. That's why you went there on your day off, to retrieve the evidence. All totaled, you did a lot of things to protect yourself."

The Captain calmly crossed his muscular arms and just snickered, as Armand added with a jab, "So, you look pretty darn guilty to me, *Jack*."

McDoogal leaned intimidatingly over his desk. "It's *Captain McDoogal* to *you*, Mr. Arnolfini!" he snapped. "I was a marine, goddamn it! And over the last fifteen years, I worked my tail off to become a police captain. I've earned that respect." With a huff and a calming deep breath, the Captain reclaimed his composure, then continued, "And looks are deceiving, Mr. Arnolfini. As an astute private eye, *you*, of all people, should know that."

With unexpected poise, McDoogal leaned back in his swivel chair and lit up a cigar with is huge hand; one that Armand noticed had healed, having keenly noticed his bandaged hand in the video. After a few puffs, he said with a stream of smoke, "Okay, so I *was* at the crime scene. Big deal. I didn't commit the crime, Mr. Arnolfini. In fact, as I now recall it, on my way home that night, I saw a shadowy figure emerge out of the Poe Cottage, then he dashed into the night and disappeared. That's when I noticed the dead body on the lawn. As you've already heard, I had quite a bit to drink that night, a function in *my* honor, by the way, so I failed to report the incident." He took another puff of his cigar, then added, "So, you might have evidence of my presence there, but that's about it. No cigar for you, Mr. Arnolfini." He pointed the burning cigar at the door. "Now get out of my office!"

Armand stood up. "So, that's it, the story changes."

"Yeah, the story changes."

"If you in fact witnessed the crime moments after it occurred, why was the first thing you asked when you arrived at the crime scene 'Has any evidence been found?' rather than admitting you had been a witness?"

The Captain sprang to his feet. "I said *get out!*"

"I'll get out of your office, Captain, but not out of your face," Armand said. "Like General MacArthur, 'I *will* return!'" With that, he turned and exited the office.

Armand quick-paced over to officer Juarez's desk, and whispered, "Can you gather the video footage and get a forensics officer to the crime scene ASAP?"

Omar glanced at officer O'Reilly—who was busy on the phone—and nodded discreetly, as Armand scurried out the door and started up his '37 Cord.

Fifteen minutes later, Armand arrived at the Poe Cottage. He ran in, only to see Martha on her knees, scrubbing the base of the brick fireplace. Armand shouted, "Stop!"

Martha spun around, startled, and looked up. "Dear God!" she said while clutching her heart. "You scared the dickens out of me."

"Please! Get away from the fireplace," Armand instructed, as he ran up beside her and kneeled down. He pushed the can of muriatic acid away and sighed. He looked at her, relieved. "Thank God you didn't clean away all of the blood."

Martha squinted, as if Armand had dementia. "But *you* told me to clean it?"

Armand laughed. "Yes, I know. But after what I've just learned, and seeing Captain McDoogal's bandaged hand in the crime-scene video, I believe he is the killer. And this blood will prove it."

Martha was even more baffled. "But this is the blood of Tyron Daniels, the thief who stole Poe's pen."

"Yes, it is. But I suspect that several drops belong to Captain McDoogal. I have a forensics specialist on the way." He grasped her hand and helped her up to her feet.

Just then, officers Juarez and Hanley strolled in. Juarez handed Armand a copy of the video. Armand pointed to the fireplace, as Hanley opened up his kit and took samples.

The next day, Armand marched into Captain McDoogal's office, followed by officers Juarez and Hanley.

McDoogal's piercing eyes sliced across the trio like a broadsword, and eventually landed back on Armand, who said, "Well, *Jack*. As promised, I've returned."

McDoogal rolled his heated eyes, as Armand continued, "And looks are no longer deceiving. In fact, they're now based on fact—a genetic DNA fact. We have your blood sample from the Poe Cottage fireplace, where you beat Tyron mercilessly and shoved him up the chimney. And that's in addition to the potpourri of evidence I mentioned yesterday. My only remaining question is why?"

McDoogal's nostrils flared like a raging bull's as he spat, "Because I got into this line of work because of Poe's stories. And those two hoodlums were about to desecrate a sacred shrine. I'm sick of how trash like that is slowly eroding our great civilization. This city has become a shithole! The Grand Concourse was once beautiful and majestic. The Botanical Gardens and Bronx Zoo are now the only two oases in a cesspool of depravity and crime. I'm sick of it! And being drunk that night only released the pent-up frustration I've been forced to endure for many years, years of watching my home town turn into an urban urinal overrun by rats."

Armand sighed, as officers Juarez and Hanley read McDoogal his rights, while the unhinged captain looked at Armand with daggers in his eyes. "One day you'll regret this!" he grumbled as he was ushered out the door in handcuffs.

Armand stood for an odd moment alone in the captain's office. His eyes then caught a glimpse of McDoogal's impressive array of military and police citations on the wall, then peered out toward the mounting chaos, as hordes of hostile dregs were being dragged in and arrested. A profound wave of melancholy washed over him, as if the last Roman emperor watching the barbarians slowly eroding civilization. Armand blinked hard, took a deep breath, and exited the precinct.

THE FIVE AND DIME MYSTERY

Armand arrived home in Westport, Connecticut, after solving his case at the Poe Cottage Museum, and plopped on the couch in the den.

Just then, Andrea walked in. "How did everything go at the precinct?"

Armand rubbed his weary eyes. "Well, it certainly gave me pause for thought. It's troubling how all great civilizations slowly succumb to toxic forces, even those that effect the guardians of the realm." He shook his head. "Well, as I suspected, Captain McDoogal committed those brutal murders." His eyes caught a hold of Andrea's decorative bowl of potpourri. He picked it up and took a sniff. "It's kind of odd. I used the word *potpourri* when explaining the wealth of evidence that mounted against him. I guess it was subliminal." He scratched his chin. "Perhaps I should call that case the Poe-pourri Mystery."

Andrea chuckled. "Very cute and poetic. I'm sure Edgar would have approved." She glanced over her shoulder. "Well, I'd like you to meet Shirley Taylor. She's an old friend of mine."

Shirley walked into the den and toward Armand, who rose to his feet. She reached over the coffee table and shook his hand. "Hello, Armand. Andrea has told me a lot about you."

"All lies, I'm sure," he said, recognizing Shirley as a TV psychic, as well as sensing that his wife was roping him into another case. "I gave up P.I, work, Shirley," he said in jest, but also hoping to test her abilities. "So, I don't know what Andrea told you."

Shirley smiled. "Evidently, you have extra sensory perception yourself, Armand. Because you *do know* what she told me. That's why I'm here. I need your help."

"Yes, you're quite right. I *do* know," he said with a sigh. "I was hoping to get a moment's rest to read, but…" he looked at Andrea. "I see my new bride is an effective saleswoman."

Andrea chuckled. "Well, I know of only one person who can handle these types of things, sweetheart."

Armand knew Andrea was pushing the envelope, making him venture into broader fields, as his recent Poepourri murder case just proved. Now with a psychic standing before him, his alleged ESP failed him, not having a clue where this was heading. He looked at Shirley, and asked with trepidation, "Okay. S-soo, how can *I* possibly help a psychic celebrity, like *you*?"

Shirley smiled. "Well, I can certainly see that you're skeptical about my abilities, Armand. But don't worry, I'm used to that." She sat in the recliner across from the couch.

"Please, have a seat. Relax, Armand. I promise I won't invade your mental space."

Armand laughed. "That's very kind of you, Shirley." He sat down. "Can I get you a drink…" he smiled, "or do I need not even talk, as I'm sure you knew what I was going to ask, right?"

Shirley chuckled. "No, Armand. My particular visions come randomly. I don't control them as much as they control me. And the visions I've been seeing over the past week have me perplexed."

"Perplexed. Okay. I like puzzles." He rubbed his hands together. "I'm ready. Let's see if I can help you unravel them."

"Excellent!" she said. "That's what I was hoping for."

Just then, Andrea interjected. "You see, honey, this is all really quite harmless. No murders, just visions to decipher."

Armand looked at his wife with a knowing smile, sure that this meeting would lead somewhere quite unexpected and beyond solving just a mere puzzle. "Yes, whatever you say, dear."

Andrea chuckled. "Fine. Then, I'll get you both something to drink and nosh on."

With that, she spun around and walked toward the kitchen.

Armand looked back at Shirley. "I hope this information isn't sensitive or top secret, because I don't have a Cone of Silence."

Shirley laughed. "No, Mr. Smart, that won't be necessary."

Armand smiled. "Okay, excuse my levity. So, tell me about this vision?"

"Well, for the past week, I've had this recurring vision of a set of architectural plans…blueprints for a skyscraper."

Armand squinted. "A skyscraper? What kind of skyscraper?"

Shirley shook her head. "I don't know, I have no architectural background, so I don't know how to describe it, other than it being very tall."

Armand walked over to his bookshelf and returned with a book on architecture. He sat back down on the couch and opened the book on the coffee table, then spun it around for her viewing. "Take a look at these buildings and see if any strike a resemblance."

Shirley leaned over and thumbed through the book. As she did, Armand said, "Is it modern, like the Twin Towers? Or perhaps an older style, like the Empire State Building?"

As Shirley continued to flip through the pages, she replied, "Yes, more like the Empire State Building, but more ornate and older looking at the top." She peered up into his eyes. "Kind of like an old cathedral. You know, like the ones in Europe during medieval times."

Armand reached over. "Excuse me," he said as he flipped several pages. "You mean like this?" He pointed to The Cathedral Building in Oakland, California.

Shirley's eyes widened. "Yes! Something like that." But as she looked closer, she said, "Oh, but it's not quite the same as my vision."

Armand flipped another page. "How about this one?" He pointed to the Tribune Tower, the neo-gothic skyscraper, built in Chicago in 1925.

Shirley's shoulders sank. "No, not that one either."

The Cathedral Building   The Tribune Tower

Just then, Andrea entered the den and placed drinks and appetizers on the coffee table. She glanced at both of them. "How are you coming along?"

Shirley shook her head. "Not so good. These buildings all look somewhat similar to me."

As Armand skimmed through the book, Shirley rubbed her chin. "Oh yes, I failed to mention, the drawing of the skyscraper I see was celebrated...for some special reason. Just what, I don't know."

Armand looked up at her. "Ah!" he said, as he touched his temple like a seer. He flipped several pages. "You must mean *this one*, yes?"

Shirley looked down at the photo. "*Yes*! That's it!" she exclaimed. "Very good, Armand." She looked up into his eyes. "Dear me, I think I have competition. How on Earth did you know that?"

Armand picked up a rolled-up piece of prosciutto. "Because the Woolworth Building was the tallest building in the world for seventeen years, from 1913 to 1930." He looked down admiringly at the photo. "It's 792 feet tall, and held that honor until the Chrysler Building knocked it off its pedestal."

Shirley looked over at Andrea and smiled. "What a relief, to finally know what building I've been seeing."

Armand took a bite of the prosciutto, then followed that with a green olive and a cube of provolone cheese. He leaned back into the sofa. "Well, Shirley, I'm glad that mystery was solved. Now I can relax."

"Oh, no!" she said. "You can't. That's just the beginning. You see, I've also been receiving ominous feelings about this architectural drawing. Something dark surrounds this building's plans. Are you aware of anything significant or sinister about them? Or perhaps about the architect?"

"Not that I'm aware of," he said. "To my knowledge, Cass Gilbert was the architect, and nothing unusual transpired between him and the owner, Frank Woolworth."

"Andrea told me you're an aficionado of several genres of fine art, but I wasn't aware you knew so much about architecture."

"Well, it goes hand-in-hand. Architecture is an art form of engineering; one I find fascinating. Filippo Brunelleschi was the Renaissance architect who studied the long-lost techniques of the master builders of ancient Rome, and by adding his own genius to the mix he truly ignited a rebirth in architecture. As the discoverer of linear perspective, Brunelleschi also enabled all future architects and visual artists to create realistic 3-D renderings, like the one I imagine you've been seeing in your visions."

"Yes," Shirley said, as her eyes veered back down at the book. "It looked very much like this photo." She looked back up at Armand. "But what about Frank Woolworth? Was he involved in some type of a scandal?"

"Not that I'm aware of," Armand said as he picked up and ate a slice of dried sausage. He swallowed, and said,

"So, this doesn't give me any leads, Shirley. I'm as lost as you are. Is there anything else you can think of that might offer a clue as to what your dark feeling is about?"

Shirley's shoulders sank as she picked up a cracker and dipped it into the spinach dip. She paused, then looked at Armand. "Not really." She inserted the cracker in her mouth and began to chew.

As Armand and Andrea looked on, Shirley sat chewing away, her eyes in a dead stare. Then, suddenly, she broke her trance and looked down at the photo of the Woolworth Building. "Wait!" she exclaimed, as she swallowed the remnants of her cracker and dip. She looked up at Armand. "How about we all go to the Woolworth Building? Perhaps being inside the building itself will prompt another vision."

Andrea interjected, "That's a splendid idea!"

Armand glanced at his wife and rolled his eyes. "Sweetie, Shirley had a *vision* of architectural plans, and a *feeling* of something sinister. It's all very nebulous and cryptic. I can't see anything tangible that would warrant an investigation."

He looked at Shirley. "No pun intended about my not being able to *see* anything, because I truly can't. And neither can you, at least not anything concrete that would lead us to believe there was actually some sort of wrongdoing."

Andrea stepped closer. "Honey, that's why we need more information. And to get that, we should go to the Woolworth Building to see if we can find that vital clue."

"Andrea, I'm accustomed to starting an investigation with some type of legitimate occurrence, not some whimsical dream or a gut feeling." He looked at Shirley, whose sullen face reeked of disappointment. Armand sighed. "Okay, Okay! I'll tell you what; to humor you, I *will* go with you to the Woolworth Building."

Shirley's face illuminated. "That's swell! Thank you!"

He added, "But it's more so to get a firsthand look at this landmark building that I never had the good fortune of visiting." As Shirley's smile withered, Armand continued, "Because, so far, this appears to be a five and dime wild goose chase."

Shirley looked at him, insulted. "Five and dime? Is that what you think of my abilities?"

Armand had to chuckle. "Shirley. While I'm not totally sold on your powers of vision, I was referring to Frank Woolworth. He was the pioneer who started the Five and Dime business model."

"Oh, I see."

"Yes, I imagine you would," Armand said, making Shirley smile.

He then looked at Andrea. "And since you're pregnant, why don't you stay here and relax? You also have work at the museum tomorrow."

"Honey, I'm pregnant, not disabled."

"Yes, I know that, sweetie. But, as I said, there's nothing concrete about this cumulous lead. We'll only be there an hour or so. I have research to do tonight for that seminar I've been asked to do at Yale."

Andrea sighed. "Okay, very well," she said as she collected the plates on the coffee table.

With that, Armand and Shirley hopped in his '57 Ford Thunderbird and headed toward Manhattan.

Arriving at the Woolworth Building, Armand and Shirley gazed up at the towering neo-gothic structure.

"It *is* quite beautiful," Shirley said. She looked back down at Armand. "So, you said this was the tallest building in the world for quite some time, yes?"

"For seventeen years," Armand said, as he admired the building's ornate gothic details. "Oddly enough, when the Chrysler Building knocked it off its pedestal in 1930, it held the title for only eleven months, until the Empire State Building snatched it, and held on to it for forty years. That's when the title was handed over to the World Trade Center's twin towers."

Shirley was impressed. "You're a walking encyclopedia."

"Well, only about the things that fire my passions and inspire me." He looked at the entrance. "Shall we go inside?"

"Certainly!"

As they entered the lobby, they both gasped. The lobby was breathtaking, with a high-coffered ceiling, grand arches, and intricate gothic detailing. "Dear me," Shirley said. "This feels like we're in a European palace. It's magnificent!"

"Indeed it is," Armand said. "This building was recently awarded New York City landmark status, so thank God it will never be demolished." As his eyes soaked in the lobby's beauty, he added, "It's a shame how many beautiful old buildings have been razed to the ground to make way for mundane boxes of steel and glass. It's critical that we keep some of these old gems alive."

Shirley spun around, trying to take in all the intricate craftsmanship, when a young guard approached them. "Excuse me," he said. "But this building is closed to the public."

Armand stepped closer toward the young man dressed in a fancy uniform. "This happens to be Shirley Taylor. Perhaps you've seen her on TV?"

The chipper guard looked closer. "Holy cow! Awesome!" he said, staring at her. "You're *The Salient Psychic*! Can I get your autograph? I watch your show all the time."

Shirley smiled. "Well, what would you like me to sign?"

He searched his pockets and pulled out a torn piece of paper with his to-do list on one side. "Well, this will have to do," he said, as he pulled a pen out of his jacket pocket. "My name is Nathan, Nathan Hanson."

As Shirley obliged, Armand interjected, "Listen, Nathan, we'd like to take a few minutes to go through the building. Shirley saw a vision, and—"

"No problem," Nathan cut in. "For Shirley the psychic, it would be my pleasure. Just keep a low profile." He looked down at the signed scrap of paper she handed back to him. "Thank you, Mrs. Taylor!" Enthusiastically, his eyes veered back up at her. "Can you tell me what my future holds for me?"

Shirley smiled. "No, I'm sorry, Nathan." She handed him a business card. "But call me, perhaps we can do a session. I'll even do the first one for free."

Nathan's eyebrows rose. "Awesome! Thank you."

Shirley's head spun around. "But I need to get some vibrations from this building, so I'd love to get started."

Nathan extended his arm toward the huge flight of stairs. "Be my guest. Just don't tell anyone I let you in."

Armand and Shirley nodded then started walking up the grand staircase, as Nathan called out in a loud whisper, "And remember...mum's the word!"

They both chuckled as Armand said, *"Mum* it is!"

Armand and Shirley toured the impressive building for over twenty minutes, going from one floor to another, when Armand finally inquired, "Well? Did you get any vibes or visions yet?"

Shirley shook her head, disappointed. "Nothing yet."

Forty minutes later, after touring most of the building, Armand asked again, receiving a sullen smirk of utter dejection, as Shirley moaned, "I don't understand it. I thought for sure I would have received some type of message. But nothing, nothing at all." She looked around her at the lavish interior, then back at Armand. "I guess you were right, this turned out to be a five and dime wild goose chase. I'm sorry, Armand."

"Don't worry, Shirley," Armand said, as his eyes glanced at the beautiful architecture. "This has been a wonderful experience. I'm glad we came."

Just then the building manager hurriedly approached them, and barked, "What are you doing in the building? Did my guard let you in?"

"No," Armand said quickly. "We're the guilty ones, we snuck past him."

The manager rubbed his chin. "Well, that's good to hear, because I was contemplating making Nathan head of security."

Shirley jumped in, "By all means, you should. Don't let us ruin his chances for a promotion. He had no way of seeing us sneak in."

It finally struck the manager that the woman before him was a TV sensation. "Ah!" he said. "You're Shirley, *The Salient Psychic*." His demeanor changed from a belligerent bulldog to a polite poodle, as he smiled graciously. "It's an honor to meet you." He squinted. "But why are you here? Is there some paranormal activity or something serious I should know about?"

Shirley glumly shook her head. "No, there's nothing to worry about. I thought I had something, but it turned out to be a false alarm." She glanced around. "But this building is magnificent. You're lucky to work in such a beautiful environment."

"Yes, lucky indeed," the manager said. "Construction of this masterpiece began on November of 1910. It cost Mr. Woolworth *thirteen and a half* million dollars, which in today's market would be about *three hundred* million dollars."

Armand shook his head in wonderment. "Wow! Thirteen and a half million would only get about two and three-quarter floors built today."

The manager paused a moment to calculate, as his eyes and lips moved with each mathematical computation. Finally, he nodded. "Yes, very good!" He looked at Armand. "That's about right. Only two and three-quarter floors out of sixty." He extended his hand and shook Armand's. "My name is Douglas Applebee. And who might you be? Her producer?"

Armand smiled. "No." He glanced at Shirley. "I'm sure she wouldn't want *me*—a skeptic—as her producer. I'm Armand Arnolfini, a private eye."

Mr. Applebee squinted, now curious, as his eyes veered back and forth between the two. "I'm getting a bad feeling. Are you sure there isn't something dreadful here that I need to know about?"

"No," Shirley said. "You see, I had a vision of the blueprints of this building, yet it was accompanied by a feeling, a premonition that something might have gone wrong. Just what that is, I'm unclear. But I sense this all took place in the past. So there's nothing relevant to the current state of affairs, Mr. Applebee."

Douglas sighed. "Thank God for that," he said. "I'm a firm believer in psychic phenomena. My brother is a colonel in the army, and he told me the Defense Intelligence Agency seriously uses such people like you, Shirley, for reconnaissance and other tactical operations." He looked at Armand. "And you say you're a skeptic?"

Armand raised his hands. "Yes. I confess. I'm guilty."

Shirley interjected, "Well, I haven't been too impressive here today to win him over. So, I can understand his mistrust."

Armand glanced at his watch. "Well, we didn't find anything and need to be on our way. We're sorry to bother you, Mr. Applebee."

"Oh, no bother at all," he said. "Allow me to escort you out."

As the threesome walked down the corridor, Douglas asked Shirley for her autograph, while Armand's eyes took in every architectural detail. He was intrigued by the random gargoyles that accented the gothic framework, many taking on human forms. That's when he noticed one of the pigmy-like statues featured a familiar face. He stopped in his tracks. "That's Frank Woolworth!" he exclaimed. "What a playful idea, to honor the owner as a gargoylesque statue."

Shirley and Douglas stopped and looked on, as Applebee said, "Oh, yes, there are quite a few of those here. A unique touch, indeed."

Armand's eyes widened. "By any chance, would there be one of the architect?"

"Why, yes, of course. Why do you ask?"

Armand looked at Shirley. "Because I'd like Shirley to see it, and perhaps see what you and I can't see."

"That's a splendid idea!" Shirley said.

Excited, Mr. Applebee escorted them to the floor where the grotesque parody of Cass Gilbert was located. They all looked up at the stone figure, which clutched a set of plans in one hand and a steel beam in the other, and sported clip-on spectacles.

Armand said, "Well, there he is, Shirley." He looked back up at the figure, which was a dummy support brace for the decorative ceiling. Playfully, he called out to the gargoyle, "Speak, Mr. Gilbert! Speak! Reveal your secret?"

Shirley laughed. "Very melodramatic, Armand. As you know, my visions don't work that way. I wish it were that easy. But you see..." her face suddenly blanched, as she squinted and touched her temple. "Dear me! I don't believe this, but..."

"But what?" Armand said, while Applebee echoed those words.

"I just saw a vision," she said, as she raised her other hand, motioning for them to be silent. "Give me a minute to concentrate."

As Armand and Douglas waited impatiently, Shirley closed her eyes and rubbed both of her temples. The seconds seemed like minutes and the minutes like hours, as Armand and Douglas stood mute and tingling with anticipation.

Then suddenly, Shirley opened her eyes. She looked as if she had just returned from an H.G. Wells time warp, as she blinked hard, then looked at Armand. "Dear Lord! It's right there!"

Armand looked around, seeing nothing. "Right *where*? Wait!" he said, confused. "What am I supposed to see?"

"The plans, the actual blueprints, Armand." Shirley looked back up at the gargoyle. "And they're inside that stone figure!"

"Impossible," Armand said. "Why would they be inside a gargoyle of the architect?"

Shirley shrugged. "I don't know. But like I said, there's something mysterious about these plans. Something is not right."

Applebee interjected, "Perhaps someone put them in there to conceal a secret." He looked at Armand. "I, for one, believe her."

"Well, if you believe her, would you be willing to take the gargoyle down and open it up?"

"Certainly," he replied. "As long as we gain access from the rear side and don't destroy the statue's façade, I'll take full responsibility."

With that, Mr. Applebee summoned one of his engineers, who arrived moments later and carefully dismounted the gargoyle of Cass Gilbert. As the engineer lowered the statue to the floor, they all saw a startling sight. A trap door was located on the back.

Applebee looked at Armand. "What do you think now?"

Armand swallowed hard. "I think I'm slowly becoming a believer. But the real test will be what we find inside."

As the engineer opened the rear door, all their eyes widened!

"Good God!" Applebee exclaimed, as he reached in and pulled out a set of yellowed blueprints. Excitedly, he opened them up on the polished floor, while Shirley and Armand hovered over his shoulder, marveling at the sight.

Applebee turned his head around, looking at Armand. "Well, Mr. Arnolfini, I believe this does it! Look at the date."

Armand moved around him to get a closer look. He shook his head in disbelief. "This *is* amazing!" He looked back up at Shirley. "I'm sorry for doubting you." Eagerly, he looked back down at the plans. But then his head recoiled. "Wait a minute!" he said, as he looked at Applebee. "These plans are not signed by Cass Gilbert." He pointed to the signature. "They're by Carlo Giancotta."

Applebee leaned forward, not believing his eyes. "That's impossible! Cass Gilbert designed this building. What sort of nonsense is this?"

"Perhaps that's the bad feelings I received," Shirley said. "But who is Carlo Giancotta?"

Armand shrugged. "Don't know. Never heard of him." He looked at Applebee. "Have you?"

"No," he uttered. "I'm at a loss for words."

Armand looked back down at the signature. "I wonder if this was just a bad joke by one of Gilbert's workers, or perhaps a ploy to take credit posthumously by a jealous rival." He looked closer at the signature and again was startled by what he saw. "Hold on!" he said. "Look at this!"

They each bent over and looked at the signature, but couldn't see anything more unusual than the name Carlo

Giancotta itself, as Shirley asked, "What is it? What do you see?"

"Look closer," Armand said. "It's very faint, but look between the lines of Carlo's signature."

As they did, they could see the partial remnants of a signature underneath that had been erased, with only a few letters barely visible.

"Ah! Yes," Applebee said. "It appears there was another signature underneath. It must be Gilbert's. That solves the mystery."

"No," Armand said. "I'm afraid not. The mystery has just grown deeper."

Shirley leaned closer. "Why is that? What do you see?"

Armand strained to make out the name underneath Carlo Giancotta's, as he said, "I can only make out what appears to be G.i.u...s...e... Ah! It's Giuseppe! However, I can't decipher the last name." He looked up at Applebee. "But it's definitely not Cass Gilbert."

Applebee's face turned perplexedly sullen. "What does this mean? Cass Gilbert wasn't the architect?"

"It's too early to say," Armand said. "This may have been a prank, in poor taste. But, if there was another architect who truly created these plans, then yes, this could change history. What's more baffling right now, however, is that we have two architects' signatures on here. Just who these men were needs to be deciphered first. That's even if they were architects. And one name is incomplete. So the mystery broadens."

Armand looked back down at the blueprints. "I see these were stamped on October 15, 1910." He looked up at Applebee. "When did you say construction started?"

"On November 4, 1910."

Armand folded up the plans. "Do you mind if I hold on to these, at least until this case is solved…or not?"

"By all means. You have more use for them now. And quite frankly, I hope they prove to be just a malicious prank."

Armand looked at Shirley. "Are there any other visions that can shed some light on these two other names?"

Shirley shook her head. "I'm sorry, no. I wish I had more to offer you."

Armand smiled. "You gave me more than I expected. You made me a believer, one who is now committed to this case."

She grinned. "That's fantastic!" She grasped his hand. "And let me say this; the fact that I located this hidden document already, with your help, will make for a great segment on my TV show. So, I can pay you handsomely for this investigation, Armand, and a whole lot more if it proves Cass Gilbert wasn't the architect. Or if there was some sort of scandal that occurred. That would make even bigger headlines."

Applebee chimed in, "And I'm sure the F. W. Woolworth Company would gladly chip in, Mr. Arnolfini. Anything to do with this organization's history would be well worth their investment."

"I thank you both, but right now I can't stop thinking about this baffling mystery. Thank you for your time and help, Mr. Applebee. I'll be in touch."

With that, he and Shirley exited the old skyscraper and walked to his '57 Thunderbird. With a turn of the ignition, they headed back to Westport, Connecticut.

An hour later, they walked in the door, as Andrea hurriedly approached them in the foyer. "What happened to you two?" She looked at Armand, annoyed. "You said you'd be there for only an hour or so. I was worried!"

"I'm sorry," Armand said. "We got caught up, more than I anticipated."

"Yes," Andrea said, as her eyes glanced at Shirley. "I figured that."

Shirley came to the rescue. "Stop your worrying, we have great news, Andrea. We found the architectural plans I envisioned."

Armand held up the yellowed artifact. "Here it is. Original blueprints from 1910. Better yet, it appears we have a potential scandal. It's possible that another architect designed the famous skyscraper."

Andrea's worries, and innate touch of jealousy, vanished, as she said, "Well, don't just stand there, come on in and tell me all about it!"

Taking seats in the living room, Shirley filled Andrea in on all the details, while Armand opened up the plans and stared at the signatures: Carlo Giancotta's and the mysterious Giuseppe, with no last name underneath it. He pulled out a magnifying glass and peered intently at the obscured name.

Shirley looked over. "Any luck finding out who the original architect is?"

Armand looked up. "Well, I managed to decipher the first letter of the last name. It's an 'M'." He took a pencil, held it almost parallel to the paper, and lightly rubbed the side of the graphite tip against the signature. Slowly, the impression of the author's signature slightly materialized, revealing the startling name, as Armand blurted, "Dear Lord, it's Giuseppe Mengoni!"

Andrea and Shirley glanced at each other and shrugged, as Shirley said, "Who is Giuseppe Mengoni?"

Armand just stared at the signature as he replied, "Mengoni was the pioneer who designed the Galleria Vittorio Emanuele II in Milan." He looked up at his wife and Shirley, still stunned. "The Galleria was built in 1877. It was the prototype of all shopping malls that have been built ever since. However, none have the grandeur and beauty of Mengoni's design. It was revolutionary, and featured a huge glass ceiling that covered its cross-shaped corridors with an enormous, octagonal dome at the center."

Andrea was perplexed. "I thought shopping malls were a recent concept?"

"Well, recent in America," Armand said. "But, no, Mengoni gave a whole new meaning to shopping a century before." He paused, distracted, and looked down at the plans of the Woolworth Building. "But is it possible that Mengoni designed the Woolworth Building?" He looked at the signature of Carlo Giancotta, who erased Mengoni's name and placed his name over it as the architect, then looked up. "Could Carlo Giancotta have stolen the plans from him, then sold them to Cass Gilbert?"

Andrea and Shirley walked over and looked down at the antiquated blueprints. Andrea then looked at Armand. "But why were they hidden inside that gargoylesque statue of Gilbert?"

"Not sure. Perhaps Gilbert didn't want anyone to know he didn't design the building," Armand said. "There are several possible scenarios, but at this moment, two strike me. One: Carlo Giancotta was an unsuccessful architect or a rival who stole Mengoni's plans and put his name on them, then traveled to America to sell them to Cass Gilbert, who had been hired by Frank Woolworth to build the world's tallest skyscraper. Gilbert then paid him for the plans and took credit, as most architectural firms do. Two: Carlo Giancotta was a junior architect of Mengoni's firm, who drew the plans but was not credited as the architect. In humiliation, he erased Mengoni's name, added his, then took his plans and traveled to America to make the sale on his own." Armand rubbed his bewildered head and laughed. "Or perhaps Carlo Giancotta worked at the Woolworth construction site, found these plans, altered the signatures, and stuck them inside the gargoyle of Gilbert as a hoax, to make *us*—the poor saps who found it—go nuts!"

As Shirley and Andrea laughed, Armand shook his head and looked at Andrea. "I hate to leave you alone while you're pregnant, honey, but I need to go to Milan. I have to find out if Giuseppe Mengoni designed this building, and who this mysterious Carlo Giancotta was?"

"I understand," Andrea said. "I'll be fine."

Shirley added, "Yes, and I'll keep an eye on her. You go ahead, I'm dying to know where this leads."

Armand called and made reservations, and after dinner he packed his bags.

Catching a red-eye flight on Alitalia, Armand landed in Milan the next morning and rented a car. He drove to a parking lot near the Galleria and started walking through the Piazza del Duomo with his briefcase in hand. As he did, he looked up at the magnificent Il Duomo cathedral, a gothic masterpiece that looked as if it were out of a fairy tale novel.

Armand stopped to take in the cathedral's beauty, recalling how even Leonardo da Vinci had drawn plans for the lantern tower at the apex of the majestic structure. Despite the tower being awarded to another architect, Armand was content to know that Milan was the longtime home of his idol. Milan boasted Leonardo's *Last Supper;* a science and technology museum dedicated to da Vinci; and—as Armand turned toward the large entrance of the Galleria—a statue of Leonardo, which sat at the opposite end of the Galleria's long corridor, just across the street from La Scala.

Turning left, Armand walked through the huge, arched entrance and into the Galleria's exquisite arcade. He looked up at the ceiling of glass, artistically supported by curved beams of iron, leading his eye back to the central enormous glass dome. Branching off of that, were two adjacent corridors, forming a colossal glass cross. To think that this innovative structure was built just after the American Civil

War made Armand marvel at the brainpower and technological brilliance that the Industrial Revolution engendered.

He glanced down at his Rolex watch, realizing he still had twenty-five minutes to kill before meeting with the Galleria's manager, Giacomo Servetti. He strolled in and out of a few swanky shops, then glanced at his prized watch once again; this time sparking an impulse. He perused several display cases, then purchased a Bvlgari Serpenti Bracelet Ladies Watch for Andrea. After shelling out $7,000.00, he grasped the precious watch, stuck it in his briefcase, and made his way to Giacomo Servetti's office on the top floor.

As he entered his office, Armand's eyes were drawn to the large window behind Giacomo, giving a splendid view of the Galleria's glass ceiling and the tastefully ornate building facades underneath, featuring a string of fine shops and eateries along the first floor.

Servetti noticed Armand's distracted gaze and smiled. "Quite beautiful. *Si, Senore* Arnolfini?"

"Yes, indeed," Armand said as he shook Giacomo's hand. "Giuseppe Mengoni created quite a dazzling feat of engineering here, one that brilliantly achieved both practical and aesthetic ends." As his eyes devoured all the fine details, he added, "And it still looks brand new."

"We try our best to keep it well maintained," Giacomo said. "My family have been caretakers of this facility for generations, so we treat it as if our own." He pointed to a small ornate couch. "Please, have a seat."

Armand sat down, and said, "Well, I'm glad to hear you have a long connection with this place, because—as I alluded to on the phone—I am very curious to know about Giuseppe Mengoni's work, beyond the Galleria. Specifically, had he ever designed a gothic-styled skyscraper?"

"Well, skyscrapers weren't invented yet during Mengoni's lifetime," Giacomo said, as he walked over to a bookshelf and slid out a large portfolio. "He died in 1877, some five to ten years before height became a goal for architects." He walked over to Armand, sat beside him, and opened the large folder. He skimmed through several pages, then stopped. "However, being a pioneer, Mengoni did toy with a fanciful concept shortly before he died, which could have been the first skyscraper."

As he pointed to the old photograph of Mengoni's design, he added, "This building would have been 450 feet tall. At that time, cathedrals held the record for tallest buildings, as most cities refused to allow secular structures to be taller than sacred ones. But clearly, Mengoni was experimenting with height for commercial purposes."

Armand glanced down at the portfolio. "Are all of Mengoni's designs accounted for in this folder?"

"No, I'm afraid not," Servetti said. "We're aware that several drawings had disappeared, either around the time of his death, in 1877, or soon after."

"Well, I'll get right to the point," Armand said as he opened his briefcase and pulled out the mysterious blueprints. "I recently came in possession of these plans. They're of the Woolworth Building in New York, and quite astonishingly, they bear Mengoni's signature." He pointed to the two signatures. "If you look close enough, you can see Giuseppe's name under Carlo Giancotta's."

As Servetti leaned closer, Armand added, "I'd like to know if you think Mengoni's signature is authentic?"

Giacomo strained to make out the partially obscured name, then looked up at Armand, shocked and bewildered. "That's his signature, all right. But, how can this be?"

"I don't know. That's why I'm here. I was hoping you'd have some type of a record documenting these plans."

"No, nothing," Servetti said. "Certainly nothing this monumental. There was speculation that Mengoni had designed a few other novel buildings before he died, but not a historic building like the Woolworth. Now I understand why you asked me about skyscrapers."

Armand sighed. "I was hoping you'd have tangible documentation for confirmation. Equally baffling is the name of Carlo Giancotta, who evidently tried to take credit for it. Do you happen to know if Carlo was an associate or rival architect of Mengoni's?"

Giacomo shook his head, still shocked by the revelation, but managed to respond: "Carlo Giancotta? No. The name doesn't ring a bell. I'm sorry. But I do have some old architectural journals, books, and directories on my shelf. You're welcome to go through them."

Armand thanked Servetti and, without delay, dove into Giacomo's treasure trove. Eagerly, his eyes skimmed the texts as his fingers flipped the pages. After twenty minutes or so, he hit pay dirt. "I've found him!" Armand said with a grin, as he looked over at Giacomo. "Carlo Giancotta was registered as an architect. There are only two small residential homes accredited to him, neither very impressive. He apprenticed under Mengoni for only three months, then operated his own business. But it says here that he was perpetually in debt and declared bankruptcy in 1909."

Servetti nodded. "It figures. Like I said, I never heard of him."

Armand looked back at the book and read more, when suddenly, his eyes widened! He gazed at Servetti. "Listen to this; it says Carlo Giancotta was killed in a brawl in New York City in 1910! That puts him near the Woolworth Building and right near the start of construction."

"That's more than a coincidence."

"It certainly is," Armand said. "Do you have a telephone directory?"

"Yes, it's right behind you. But who do you intend to call?"

Armand grasped the phone book. "I intend to locate relatives of Carlo Giancotta. I need to know more about this cretin. Because I suspect that he stole the plans from Mengoni and sold them to Cass Gilbert, who in turn took credit from Carlos, who in reality took credit from Mengoni."

Servetti scratched his head. *"Madonna mi!* That's one crazy cascade of crime."

Armand chuckled. *"Si, Senore* Servetti. But in Gilbert's case, I suspect he bought the plans legitimately. As most firms do, they take credit for whatever they purchase. Fair, it's *not*, but it's the ugly way of big business. Besides, this is only one theory, but the one I aim to follow first." He scanned the phone book and found six Giancottas in Milan. "May I use your phone?"

"By all means," Servetti said, pointing to the one on his desk.

Armand started to ring each of the numbers, and on the fourth call, he struck a winner. He thanked Giacomo and dashed back to his rented car. Twenty minutes later, Armand arrived at the home of Pasquale and Anna Giancotta, an elderly couple in their eighties with two married children. After a round of introductions and pleasantries, Armand was escorted into the living room, where they all sat down, as Armand said, "Well, as I alluded to over the phone, I'm trying learn more about your distant relative Carlo. I know he was an architect, and even studied under Giuseppe Mengoni for a short spell. But can you tell me anything else?"

Pasquale's old squinty eyes widened with delight as he seized the moment with gusto. "Ah! Yes, Carlo was my great grandfather. He was a genius! A fantastic architect." Pasquale's demeanor suddenly turned bitter as he continued, "A genius who never caught a break, that is." He slapped the arm of his chair. "*Senore* Mengoni didn't appreciate Carlo. Jealousy, I say! Carlo was a gifted youth, one that could have surely surpassed his master, if given a chance. But he was fired, and roadblocks plagued his life, until that dreadful day when Carlo's life was cruelly snatched away from him."

Armand had been discreetly studying Pasquale's expressions and delivery, while also observing Anna's dour expression, where she even rolled her eyes when Pasquale graced Carlo with the word 'genius'. Armand looked at Pasquale straight in the eye. "Why do you say Carlo was a genius?"

Pasquale puffed up his old, sunken chest and said with pride, "Because he designed the tallest building in the world, *that's why*!"

Armand nearly choked. He wasn't ready to hear such a remark. Evidently, Carlo had bamboozled his kin, not to mention everyone else he met. Armand kept a straight face as best he could, and asked, "Really? And what building might that be?"

"The Woolworth Building, in New York City," Pasquale said, as Anna once again discreetly turned her head and rolled her eyes.

Armand's lips puckered. "Really? The Woolworth Building? But that was designed by Cass Gilbert."

Pasquale's demeanor changed once again, this time as quickly as a sassy cat's, as he hissed through his old rotted teeth, "That's bunk! Do you hear me? *Bunk*!" Pasquale's aged body quaked as he continued his charge, "My great grandfather was robbed of his brilliant design as well as his fortune and fame. Then some grubby, two-bit steelworker in America pushed him off a building and killed him! It was a tragedy. Do you hear me? A damn tragedy! *And* a mockery of justice!"

Pasquale's bony chest heaved as he gasped for air. Anna reached over and patted his knee. "Pasquale, *calmati*, easy. Your heart."

Pasquale glanced at his wife and nodded irritably as he took deep breaths and held his heaving chest.

Armand stood up. "I'm sorry, Pasquale. I didn't mean to offend or upset you. Thank you for your time. I'll take my leave."

Pasquale choked and wiped his salivary mouth with a wrinkled handkerchief, then looked at Armand and pointed at him with his gnarly finger. "You mark my words, *Senore* Arnolfini. Carlo Giancotta will one day rise from the ashes and be hailed as the great man and architect he was!"

Anna quickly rose to her feet and grasped Armand's hand. "Please, I will show you out."

As they walked down the hallway, Anna looked up at Armand. "Don't mind him. He always defends Carlo and his family name. My maiden name was Anna Sangallo. And my family didn't take kindly to me marrying into the Giancotta clan."

"Why was that?"

Anna stopped and held Armand's hand tighter. She glanced back toward the living room, then back at Armand, and whispered, "Carlo was a brash and bitter louse. Constantly broke, and always scheming to make money or a famous name for himself. Even if it meant by stealing."

Again, she glanced at the living room, and added, "Personally, I think Carlo got what he deserved."

Armand expected to hear a conflicting tale, but not one this damning. He looked at Anna and kissed her on the forehead. "*Grazie*. I appreciate your candor, Anna. It confirms my suspicions."

With that, Armand exited the house, while Anna stood by the door and rubbed her forehead with a subtle smile.

Armand caught the next plane and landed in La Guardia Airport the next day. He drove home to Westport, Connecticut, and embraced Andrea. He looked deep into her eyes. "I missed you. But I need to ask; what do you think of my family?"

Andrea squinted. "What do you mean?"

"I mean, the Arnolfinis. What do you think of my kin?"

Andrea laughed. "You know I love your family, from you and your dad, all the way back to the famous Arnolfini in van Eyck's painting. You all make a very attractive and artistic package."

As Armand smiled, Andrea added, "Correction; in van Eyck's case, your distant relative wasn't very attractive, but the overall picture *was* very artistic...a masterpiece, in fact."

Armand giggled. "Fair enough."

Andrea squinted. "But, what's this all about?"

"Oh, nothing. Just a silly test, to make sure my perspective is clear." With that, he pulled out the $7,000 Bvlgari Serpenti Bracelet Watch, grasped her hand, and slid the serpent-like gold watch on her wrist. As Andrea's eyes bulged, he said, "And don't take this as a bribe. I love you madly!"

Andrea smiled, then embraced him warmly and kissed him lovingly on the lips. "Madly, huh? I think that trip made you a little mad. This had to cost a fortune."

"You're worth it."

"Don't ever forget that," Andrea said with a giggle. She gazed at the finely crafted detail of the sparkling gold watch, appreciating Armand's thoughtfulness and fine taste, yet knowing that even a Timex would have sufficed, as bling could never trump the string that connected their hearts. Lovingly, she looked up at Armand. "Thank you, sweetheart. It wasn't necessary, but it's truly gorgeous. I love it." As she set the time, she prodded, "Now, what happened in Milan?"

He walked over and sat down on the couch. "Well, Giuseppe Mengoni's signature on the Woolworth plans was authenticated. And before he died, he had been designing— what in several years would be deemed—skyscrapers. As for Carlo Giancotta, well, he turned out to be the low-life wannabe I suspected."

Andrea sat across from him in a recliner. "So, Carlo stole the plans from Mengoni, then put his name on it and sold it to Cass Gilbert?"

"It appears so," Armand said. "At least at this juncture. But some thirty years transpired between Mengoni's death in 1877 and the start of constructing the Woolworth Building in 1910. So, it bothers me that Carlo would have held onto a vital set of plans for so long. For a guy who was struggling to make ends meet, it just doesn't add up. Something is missing from the puzzle."

Wearily he rubbed his eyes and sunk deeper into the couch.

Andrea got up. "You relax. I'll go make us a nice cup of tea, okay?"

Armand waved tepidly as he closed his eyes. "Yes, thank you, sweetheart."

As Andrea walked into the kitchen, Armand's eyes sprang open! He leapt to his feet, ran to his bookshelf, and pulled out his book on architecture. He flipped the pages until he came to the Mengoni chapter, then scanned it quickly, coming to the info he had suddenly recalled.

As Andrea walked back in with a plate of cookies, he said, "Oh, my!"

She placed the cookies on the coffee table. "What's up?"

Armand looked at her, almost in a trance. "Not what's *up*…more like, what went *down*."

"What do you mean?"

Armand snapped the book shut. "Do you happen to know how Giuseppe Mengoni died?"

Andrea shrugged. "No."

"He fell off the roof of the Galleria while under construction."

"Oh, dear!" Andrea said with a gasp. "That's terrible. And?"

"And, I think Carlo might have pushed him off."

"Murder!?" Andrea exclaimed as her hand clutched her chest. "Why would he do that?"

Armand picked up the phone. "Because he wanted Mengoni's plans of the Woolworth Building to sell and get his miserable life out of debt. And from what Anna Giancotta said about him, I believe Carlo would do anything to get them—even murder. This sounds like a bitter and depressed man hellbent on fame and fortune." He dialed his friend at police headquarters in lower Manhattan, and setup a meeting for the next day.

At 8AM Armand walked into Inspector Warren Halifax's office. "Warren, good to see you," Armand said as he shook his hand. "Thanks for taking the time to see me."

"Always a pleasure, Armand," Halifax said as he took a seat behind his cluttered desk. "How can I help you?"

"I'd like access to your archives. I'm looking into a case pertaining to the Woolworth Building and it's alleged architect, Cass Gilbert."

Halifax squinted. "Alleged? I can save you a trip, Armand. Gilbert not only designed the Woolworth Building but also the New York Life Building, and they both still stand today. I thought *you* certainly would have known that?"

Armand smiled. "Yes, of course, Warren. But you see, I came across some disturbing evidence that indicates otherwise. So, I just would like to follow this trail to its conclusion, if possible."

"Do you mind if I ask how you came about this information?"

Armand smiled. "Well, don't laugh, but it came by means of a vision."

"A vision?"

"Yes. From Shirley Taylor, the TV psychic. She saw a vision of the blueprints of the Woolworth Building. We visited the site, but she had no vibes, so she said. Evidently, my fascination with the building's unique gargoyles led us to the one of Cass Gilbert, where the plans were concealed inside of it, which Shirley then envisioned."

"Actually, a few years ago, I would have laughed," Halifax said. "But I believe it. We've been implementing psychics into our own investigations. Naturally, it's hit and miss, mostly miss. But when one of them does nail something down, it *is* quite impressive."

Armand nodded. "I didn't believe this nonsense myself, until I was proven wrong. There are far more mysteries about the human brain than I imagined."

"Indeed, like why so many people are murderers, rapists, or pedophiles. There's a dark side that still baffles the hell out of us." Halifax looked deep into Armand's eyes. "But what prompted an esteemed P.I., like *you*, to investigate a Woolworth Building matter. It's not only old news but just a five and dime case."

Armand chuckled. "Yes, that's what I initially thought, too, but there seems to have been a scandal that took place, and I aim to uncover it."

"Okay, whatever," Halifax said as he picked up the phone. "Give me a minute." He dialed the archive director and Jack Lowell answered. Halifax told Jack to expect a friend of his, and to give him full access.

Armand thanked Warren and headed downstairs. He met Jack, who authorized Armand's entry, who then stepped into the secure room, with its endless rows of tall cabinets and several microfilm terminals.

Jack pointed to a new computer that was just installed, and said, "We just got this baby. It's a Commodore Amiga and has 512 kilobytes of memory. It's a powerhouse! This computer revolution will surely change things. Hopefully we'll get all this data on hard drives one day, but for now, you'll have to go through the paper folders and microfilm."

Armand nodded. "No problem, Jack. I'll manage. Thanks."

Armand searched and, sometime later, found a folder containing reports about Cass Gilbert, the Woolworth Building, and the police report of Carlo Giancotta's death. As he flipped through the manila folder, he saw a roll of microfilm next to it. He placed the microfilm into the terminal, and scrolled until he came upon the official police report. It was entered by police officer, Sergeant John O'Hara. As Armand's eyes scanned and read O'Hara's report, his pulse quickened with each scroll of text on the monitor, drawing him back in time, which read:

I arrived at the construction site at 7:43 AM, November 22, 1910, after receiving a call from Mr. Cass Gilbert, the building's architect. I found the body of Carlo Giancotta, an Italian citizen and architect, lying on the sidewalk. He was severely injured but still alive. I ordered officer Bill Daniels to assist the medics, who arrived at 7:45 AM, while I questioned Mr. Gilbert.

Cass Gilbert explained that Carlo Giancotta had visited his office six months prior looking for a job. Mr. Gilbert hired Mr. Giancotta, who several weeks later stole his blueprints of the Woolworth Building, which Gilbert had recently finished, save for his signature. Evidently, Carlo Giancotta forged Giuseppe Mengoni's signature on the blueprints with the intent of selling them directly to Mr. Frank Woolworth, believing Mengoni's respectable name carried the necessary clout to make the sale. However, Carlo had a change of heart, and decided he wanted not only the lucrative contract, but also the glory of receiving credit for what I was told will soon be the tallest building in the world.

However, Mr. Giancotta's ham-fisted ploy backfired. Despite approaching Mr. Woolworth first with the finished set of plans, Mr. Woolworth was soon alerted to the scam by Mr. Gilbert.

Carlo Giancotta was enraged and came to the construction site this morning with a crowbar to injure or kill Mr. Gilbert, who was performing an inspection on the unfinished second story of the building. Carlo charged Gilbert, but a steelworker, by the name of Ned Devlin, intervened. Mr. Devlin informed me that a struggle ensued and that during the scuffle, Carlo attempted to kill him, but lost his footing and accidentally fell. Mr. Gilbert and twenty other eyewitnesses at the scene corroborated Devlin's report. By the look in their eyes, I suspect they were all telling the truth, and that Mr. Devlin was merely defending himself and the honor of Mr. Gilbert.

Less than an hour later, I learned that Carlo Giancotta died at St. Gregory's Free Emergency Accident Hospital and Ambulance Station at 8:33AM. This case is now officially closed.

Armand leaned back and just stared at the screen. He knew Carlo Giancotta was a belligerent brute and a failed architect, who was down on his luck. But to think he could pull off a scheme like this and try to kill Gilbert and Devlin was truly the highlight of his pathetic life. Armand glanced down at the manila folder. His eyes caught another folder, with the initials "CG" on it. Whether it pertained to Cass Gilbert of Carlo Giancotta, he wasn't sure, but that their initials jived came as an odd coincidence. He picked it up and opened it.

It was the hospital report for Carlo Giancotta. Armand scanned the sheet, seeing the standard notations and readings of Carlo's vitals. He flipped the page to peruse more of the same, then tossed it back into the folder. As it landed, he noticed a handwritten note on the back of the report. Intrigued, he picked it back up. A nurse had recorded the note.

My name is nurse Caroline Beckman. I was entrusted with the care of Mr. Carlo Giancotta, who entered the hospital mortally injured. At 8:29 AM Mr. Giancotta made his last confession on his deathbed. He looked at me and said:

"I regret stealing Mr. Gilbert's plans, and for the terrible thing I did to Giuseppe. He was my mentor, but hurt me dearly. He said I had no future as an architect and should seek another profession. It appears now that he was right."

At that moment, Mr. Giancotta turned away from me and looked up at the ceiling, and cried mournfully:

"Giuseppe, forgive me. I was an animal, a jealous madman when I pushed you off the roof of your masterpiece. It was a vain attempt to literally dethrone you from atop that glorious dome, symbol of the lofty heights you had achieved through hard work, sheer genius, and a quest for modernization. You were right. I was nothing, a flimsy facade without a core. Destined to crumble, I'm a ruin, soon to be nothing. Gone without a trace...for all eternity. As it should be."

Mr. Giancotta died seconds later. I have no idea who the aforementioned Giuseppe might be, but it's a bizarre twist of fate that Carlo killed a man by pushing him off of a roof and was condemned to die himself in a similar fashion. Murder—borne out of greed and envy—had gone full circle.

A chill ran down Armand's back. He sat for several minutes, just soaking in the convoluted chain of events. Then, he thanked Jack Lowell and left.

An hour later, Armand arrived home, as Andrea greeted him: "So, how did it go?"

Armand shook his head. "Well, to be honest, it was quite eerie."

"How so?"

He looked deep into her eyes. "I got more than I expected. I received a chilling confession from Carlo Giancotta."

Andrea's head recoiled. "From Carlo? Honey, are you telling me that you're a psychic now, like Shirley, hearing voices from the dead?"

Armand managed to chuckle. "No, dear. Not at all. I—"

"But, Carlo died a long time ago," she cut in.

"Yes, he did. But on the back of his death certificate his nurse recorded his last confession. I'm telling you, it was very eerie, as if Carlo were speaking directly to me."

"Dear me!" Andrea said as they each took a seat in the living room. "So, what did he say?"

"He confessed to killing Giuseppe Mengoni. He pushed him off the dome of the Galleria. Mengoni didn't fall accidentally. That changes history."

"He murdered Mengoni!?" she gasped. "That's what you suspected." She paused in thought for but a second, then added, "I'm guessing that occurred while Carlo was trying to steal Mengoni's plans of the Woolworth Building?"

Armand sighed. "No. In that regard, I was wrong. Mengoni didn't draw the plans. Gilbert did. His authorship remains intact. Carlo stole the plans from Gilbert and tried to sell them to Frank Woolworth as his own. He killed Mengoni simply because he told Carlo the truth, that he wasn't cut out to be an architect."

Andrea rubbed her temple. "Jeez, what a crazy story. And a crazy man." She looked at her husband admiringly. "But you did a fine job, sweetheart, of bringing this elaborate mystery to light." Her eyes widened. "Wait! But, didn't you say Carlo was pushed off of a building, as well?"

Armand nodded. "Yes. It truly was a bizarre chain of events. As the nurse so aptly said: 'Murder—borne out of greed and envy—had gone full circle.'" He reached over and picked up the phone. "Wait until Shirley hears about this." As he dialed the number, he added, "I'm sure she didn't *see* this coming."

AMNESIA OF ARTEMISIA

Six weeks after the Woolworth case, which Shirley Taylor presented on her TV show to great acclaim, Armand received the additional check Shirley sent to him as a bonus.

Armand turned and handed the check to Andrea. "Here, please deposit this. You should buy something nice for yourself."

Andrea grasped the check and looked at it, then back up at Armand with wide eyes. "A twenty thousand dollar bonus!?" she exclaimed.

"What can I say?" Armand said as he poured himself another cup of coffee. "That segment got very high ratings and a lot of new advertisers. Shirley said they plan on doing another episode on the Woolworth revelation, aptly entitled *The Five and Dime Mystery.*" He took a sip and added, "She even asked me to appear on the show."

"That's fantastic!" Andrea said.

Armand took a seat on the living room couch. "Naturally, I declined."

"What!? Why?" Andrea said as she scurried over and sat beside him. "That would give you high visibility, and help you get more cases, and who knows where that could lead."

"It could lead to less privacy, Andrea," Armand said. He placed his hand on her knee. "I have enough good press already in the papers and plenty of work, it's a niche market. I really have very little competition, sweetie. But more importantly, celebrity doesn't appeal to me. My work appeals to me. I saw how people barraged Shirley for autographs. That would mean any place we go we'd have no privacy: people walking up to us in a restaurant, or at a mall, or at a concert, the beach, or anywhere asking for an autograph or a photo. On top of that we'd have the paparazzi following us and journalists prying into our private lives. Is that what you'd want?"

Andrea looked down at the check, then up into his humble and sincere eyes. "No, you're right. I wouldn't want that." She reached over and tenderly held his hand. "I love you."

"And I you."

Just then the phone rang. Armand reached over to the end table and lifted the receiver. "Hello?"

The man's voice on the other end came through: "Armand, it's Bernard Higley. I hope I'm not getting you at a bad time?"

"No, not at all, Bernie. What's up?"

"Well, as you know, the Cloisters Museum caters mostly to medieval works and several early Renaissance works. However, I was recently presented with a unique find. It's a Baroque work, which I know is one of your fortes.

So, I'd like to hire you to examine the piece before I make a purchase. I learned the hard way with my debacle with the Phantom Forger, which you brilliantly solved."

Armand looked at Andrea, covered the mouthpiece with his other hand, and whispered, "You see, Bernard Higley has another job for me."

Andrea smiled and kissed him on the cheek, then placed the check on his lap and headed for the kitchen.

Armand returned to the call. "That's a wise decision, Bernie. Do you mind telling me who this Baroque artist is?"

"Orazio Gentileschi," Bernard said. "At least that's what I've been told. As I said, I'm not very familiar with Baroque artists. An associate of mine, down at the Met, said Orazio was a major player, and this new find can yield some good press and financial rewards."

"That's true," Armand said. "I have a comprehensive book on Orazio, I'll bring it with me. I can be there in forty minutes. Does that work?"

"Absolutely!" Bernard said. "I'll see you then." And he hung up.

Forty minutes later, Armand walked into the Cloisters Museum, right on time, while Bernard Higley eagerly approached him. He looked down at his watch, then up at Armand. "You're a pro, Armand: precision, perception, patience, perfection!"

Armand laughed as he shook Bernard's hand. "Well, at least you see it that way."

"Hogwash!" Bernard said. "It's not just me, Armand. That's for darn sure." He wrapped his arm around Armand and started to escort him downstairs. As they navigated through the labyrinth of corridors in the medieval complex, Bernard continued, "I was presented with this find by a man named Dominic Cafaldo. He says he's starting up an art dealership, and this will be his first transaction. Therefore, I need a professional opinion. I trust you more than some of these highfalutin art critics who claim to know more about pieces than even the artists themselves."

Armand smiled as they entered the room. "You're right at that, Bernie, many have attributed works to the wrong artists and have even authenticated forgeries. As they say, art is subjective, so it's a very difficult task to assess works. In that regard, you can't expect my judgments to always be infallible, either."

Higley nodded. "Yes, I'm aware of that, Armand. But your track record is far superior to any critic I know, so..." he pointed to the painting. "There it is!"

Armand turned toward the painting. His face winced with revulsion, then mellowed, as his eyebrows rose. Suddenly, a subtle smile emerged from his once again handsome face. Enthralled, he walked toward the masterful work.

Armand's eyes devoured the composition, as he said, "Bernie, so far, I can say this looks very impressive. Brutal, but stunning."

"Yes, I didn't know what to make of it myself upon first viewing," Bernard said. "The vast majority of our medieval and gothic works are spiritual and uplifting. So, I was aghast at this painting, until Dan Hurtz at the Met told me that the Baroque era introduced some very atrocious and realistic scenes, like this one."

Armand looked back at Bernard. "Yes, Caravaggio was the leading painter of the Baroque era. He was a volatile force, even in his personal life. He killed a man and spent time in prison. But he was a masterful painter and innovator, with no peers. His influence was extremely wide-ranging in his time and prophetically far-reaching, influencing Rembrandt, Rubens, La Tour, and countless others."

Bernard Higley smiled. "That's why I love working with you, Armand. You're a consummate tour guide, even for an art museum curator like myself."

Armand chuckled. "Well, I love what I do, Bernie."

"So, tell me," Higley said. "Is this an original Orazio Gentileschi?"

Armand glanced at the painting, and said. "I'm afraid not."

Bernard squinted. "But, your first reaction? It appeared you believed this was authentic. Why do you think it's a fake?"

"I didn't say it's a fake, Bernie. I just said it's not by Orazio Gentileschi."

"But I showed Dan Hurtz this painting just this morning. He said unequivocally that it's by Orazio Gentileschi."

"It does at first glance," Armand said. "But, there's a sad amnesia of Artemisia."

Bernard squinted. "I'm not following you. *Artemisia*? It rhymes with amnesia. Are you being linguistically playful or is that an art term related to the Baroque period?"

"No," Armand said with a chuckle. "But that's exactly what I mean."

Again, Bernard squinted. "Now I'm even more confused. What *is* Artemisia?"

"Not what is, *who* is," Armand said.

"Okay, so...*who* is Artemisia?"

"She was the daughter of Orazio—Artemisia Gentileschi. And she was an extremely gifted artist who was cast into the shadows and overlooked for centuries and, in essence, forgotten by sexist historians. Hence the amnesia of Artemisia."

Higley looked at the painting then back at Armand. "So you believe this painting is by Artemisia, not her father?"

"It appears so." Armand walked closer to the painting and pointed to the woman wielding the sword. "This is Judith. Artemisia painted very strong representations of women, especially in her several versions of *Judith and Her Maidservant Beheading Holofernes*. Which, by the way, this is." Armand opened the book in his hand and turned several pages, landing on a photo of the same disturbing scene, but painted by Orazio, and said, "As you can see, Artemisia's father painted the same scene, but he chose to picture Judith after the beheading. Judith is even looking away from the horrific act she committed."

He turned the page where Artemisia's famous rendition of the scene was presented for comparison. "Now look here," he said. "Artemisia captured Judith in the midst of the bloody beheading."

Bernard looked at the photo. His face cringed at the ghastly vision of Judith decapitating Holofernes. "Oh, dear Lord, yes. It's very much like the version I now wish to acquire." He glanced over at the painting on the easel, which was the same brutal act, but viewed from a different angle, while Armand said, "So, you see, Orazio's style was different, he opted not to capture the brutality of Judith's actions like his daughter."

"Indeed not," Bernard said, as he looked at Armand. "Forgive my naivety, Armand, but what pagan myth is this portraying?"

"Not pagan, Bernie. This is Biblical. Judith was a Jewish woman who snuck into the tent of Holofernes, an Assyrian general, who had intentions of attacking and destroying Bethulia, Judith's village."

"Ah, so I see," Bernard said. "Excuse my lapse in the Scriptures, I'm not up to snuff, as I should be." He looked back at the painting. "Well, now knowing of Judith's motive, to defend her city, it sheds a different light on things, despite this painting being literally very dark. Except for that dramatic glow of candlelight."

Armand looked back at the grim painting, occurring in the blackness of night. "Yes, the use of chiaroscuro, light and dark, especially from one light source, was a brilliant innovation by Caravaggio, one that Artemisia made very good use of here."

Bernard gazed at the sheer brutality of how Judith was in the process of cutting Holofernes' head off, with blood spurting like a fountain and soiling the white sheets. Again Bernard's throat tightened with revulsion, as he turned and looked at Armand. "People may call me a chauvinist for saying this, but I can't fathom how a tender woman could paint something so horrific like this."

"Well, Artemisia was a strong and spirited woman," Armand said. "At seventeen she was raped by Agostino Tassi, who happened to be an artist and friend of her father's. He was given free reign to tutor Artemisia, but was infatuated with her. Despite being married, Tassi took advantage of Artemisia. The sad thing is, she continued to have sexual relations with him for a year afterwards, to protect her honor. Tassi strung her along with promises of marriage, but he was a shady scoundrel, one who had done time in prison, and was even accused of allegedly having his wife murdered."

Bernard's eyes widened at the convoluted tale. "Dear Lord, what a bizarre set of circumstances."

Armand nodded. "Yes, and after a year of this peculiar courtship, Tassi refused to marry her. That prompted Artemisia's father, Orazio, to bring the rape case to court."

"A year later!?"

"Yes, as I said, it was a very peculiar event. But there's no doubt that Artemisia refused Tassi's first encounter."

"How is that?" Higley said. "It sounds like she had feelings for him."

"She might have, but arranged marriages and defending a woman's virginity were standard practices at that time. She hoped to avoid a scandal, but sex was all Tassi wanted, not marriage. He was a lecherous lowlife. Furthermore, during the trial, they bound Artemisia's hands with cords and tightened them, causing immense pain in her fingers. This torture test was supposed to induce Artemisia to tell the truth; namely, that she wasn't raped. But Artemisia said otherwise, and Tassi was sentenced to two years in prison. However, he didn't serve the full term and was released early."

Higley shook his head. "Dear Lord. What a lurid tale."

"Yes, and it's clear that the rape had some effect on her psyche while painting. In *Susanna and the Elders*, Artemisia portrays a young woman trying get away from two lecherous men scheming to abuse her."

"But perhaps more humiliating," Armand continued, "was how she constantly had to prove herself in a man's world. Artemisia certainly had the artistic skills to match her male peers, but making headway for a woman artist, especially at that time in history, was a daunting battle, one with practically impossible odds. So, between the widespread influences of Caravaggio's dramatic style, her humiliation of being raped, and suppressed by her male peers, it was a perfect recipe for a strong woman with conviction and nerves of steel to fight her way through the abuse and prejudices. And quite amazingly, Artemisia *did* manage to be successful in her day, being the first woman to do so. But, the sexist historians disregarded her. Therefore, I can't help but admire her fortitude and amazing skills."

Bernard nodded pensively as he turned and looked at the bold and utterly brutal painting. "Yes, I can now see the pain, frustration, and bitter vengeance that fueled her hands to paint this vicious act. It makes this scene even more real and harrowing."

Armand also gazed back at the painting. "Well, there have been many artists who portrayed this scene, from Michelangelo and Mantegna to Botticelli and Klimt. And of course, Caravaggio, whose earlier version is just as brutal."

Andrea Mantegna   Gustav Klimt

Armand stepped closer, examining the application of paint and glazes, as well as the aged cracks in the varnish. "But I would like to take some tiny samples, Bernie. Just to make sure."

"By all means, Armand. But you'll need to do it quickly, today. Because this new dealer, Dominic Cafaldo, only allowed me one day to inspect it, before returning it to him, or making the purchase."

Armand looked back at Bernard. "That's an awfully short timeframe. But, I'll make it happen. I have friends at the lab who can turn this around for me in a few hours."

"Excellent!" Higley said, while Armand proceeded to extract small samples of paint from the outer edges of the canvas and a tiny piece of the canvas itself.

Three hours later, Armand returned. Bernard stood with bated breath, anxiously awaiting the verdict, as Armand said, "I hate to be the bearer of bad news, Bernie, but we found traces of resin and lead, not to be found in any of Artemisia's paintings."

Higley sighed, annoyed, as he glanced back at the painting. "I can't believe I have another forgery standing before me." He looked at Armand with sad puppy eyes. "I thought for sure this was authentic. From what you told me of Artemisia, it seemed a sure winner."

"As you know, Bernie, there are plenty of very talented artists today. Many who will never gain the fame and fortunes they deserve. But the skill of painting and aging a work—by heating it in an oven or using special solvents and techniques to create believable craquelure—has grown exponentially over the centuries, so forgers can be very convincing."

"Yes, I can see," Bernard said, disappointed and humiliated. "But it irks me that these talents try to steal someone else's fame." He looked at his watch. "This Dominic Cafaldo fellow will be here any minute. Do you think he's the forger?"

"It's hard to tell. He might be, or else he's fencing it for the forger, or he has no clue it's a fake. You did say this was a new field for him, right?"

Higley nodded with a smirk. "Yes."

"Well, at least you didn't buy the painting already. So cheer up."

A warm smile graced Bernard's face. "Yes. Thank you, Armand. I owe you big time. If I'd listened only to Dan Hurtz at the Met I would have been in another mess."

Just then Dominic Cafaldo walked in wearing his expensive pinstripe suit with a black shirt, no tie, and three thick gold necklaces dangling over his hairy chest. "Yo, Mr. Higley! How are you? One of your guards escorted me down here."

As Armand and Bernard saw the guard in question take his leave, Bernard replied, "Hello, Mr. Cafaldo." He pointed to Armand. "This is Armand Arnolfini. He's not only the finest art investigator but also an eminent art expert, especially in the Renaissance and Baroque eras."

Dominic reached over and shook Armand's hand firmly, his bulky diamond and gold ring digging into Armand's palm. "Pleased to meet you."

"I don't think you will be," Armand said.

Dominic squinted. "And why's that?"

"Because your painting is a fake."

Dominic smirked and pushed his way past Armand with the back of his hand, then defensively stood by the painting, as if a father protecting his daughter. He looked at

Bernard. "He's wrong, Mr. Higley! Don't listen to him. Look at this painting. It's magnificent! How can he say it ain't authentic? It's a genuine Orazio Gentileschi. My partner in Rome even authenticated it. Your expert here is wrong! *Dead wrong!*"

"I think not," Bernard said, as Armand chimed in, "Mr. Cafaldo, even if it were authentic, you had the wrong artist's name. This style more closely fits Orazio's daughter, Artemisia."

"Bullshit!" Dominic barked. "I don't know who you are, but I purchased this painting from Sergio Lavanti, it has a clear and respectable provenance."

"Sergio Lavanti?" Armand queried. "Is he related to Luca and Filomena Lavanti?"

Dominic's head recoiled with surprise. "You know the Lavantis?"

"Yes," Armand said. "They're very wealthy collectors. My father is a friend of Luca's. Filomena, however, passed away last year. So who is Sergio?"

Dominic cracked his neck and crossed his arms. "Sergio inherited the estate. Luca died a month ago."

"But the Lavantis had no children," Armand said.

Dominic rolled his eyes. "Yeah, Sergio is their only nephew and surviving relative. Like I said, this is an original with a solid provenance." Cockily he added, "So, do you wanna change your verdict now, Mr. Arnolfini?"

Armand chuckled. "No, Dominic. I can see you're young, and Bernard tells me this is your first venture into dealing with fine art. So, I can tell you, there are plenty of forgeries in the art world, even hanging on museum walls." He glanced at the painting, then back at Dominic. "And if you'd like me to demonstrate that it's a fake, right here before your eyes, I'll gladly do so. But that will entail wiping away some of the paint and damaging the painting."

"I don't think so," Dominic said. "I know it's real. If you're willing to cough up the dough for it, you can do whatever you wish. In other words, put your money where your mouth is, Mr. Arnolfini."

"I'll tell you what," Armand said. "I'll gladly buy it, only if it's real. But if I prove it's a fake, I'll owe you nothing. It remains yours. How's that?"

Dominic nervously glanced at the painting, then at Bernard. "This ain't what I expected, Mr. Higley. I didn't come here to get involved in a gamble about its authenticity. I gave you a full day to do your evaluations. And time is up. So, I'll just take my painting and leave."

Higley shrugged. "Go ahead, Mr. Cafaldo. But be assured that I *will* put out a call to all my fellow curators and to every major auction house that it's a fake. So, you'll never be able to sell it."

Dominic's lips tightened and twisted, as he huffed. "Fine! Go ahead, Arnolfini. But be prepared to cough up the bucks."

"We'll see about that," Armand said, as he picked up a bottle of cleaning fluid and walked toward another painting nearby. "This is the fluid Bernard uses to delicately clean all of his prized possessions here at the museum." With that, Armand poured some liquid on a fine cloth, then wiped it across the old medieval painting. He allowed it time to dry, then poured another dose on the cloth and walked over to the alleged Gentileschi. "You saw how it didn't harm the other painting, but brace yourself," he said, as he wiped a lower section of the painting.

Before their eyes, the solution ate away the paint as if acid, right down to the white canvas. Dominic gasped and his eyes bulged, while Bernard smiled.

Dominic stepped up to the painting. "What the hell did you do!?" he spat, as he turned and looked at Armand with pit bull eyes. "You've ruined a masterpiece! What sort of trickery is this?"

"No trickery," Armand said. "I had small samples of paint tested at a lab." He pointed to the small specks that were removed on the outer edges of the painting. "The test results not only indicated modern materials that weren't used in the Baroque era, but they also found traces of glycerin."

Dominic's fuse was burning fast. "What the hell is glycerin?"

"Glycerin dissolves instantly when subjected to normal cleaners," Armand said. "That's why the cleaner had no effect on the other painting. As I said, you have a fake, Dominic. And I owe you nothing more than my sympathies for purchasing a forgery."

Dominic seethed as he looked at Higley, then back at Armand. "Glycerin. How the hell is that possible? And why would any artist use glycerin? It don't make sense."

"It does," Armand said, "if the forger wanted this work to be exposed as a fraud. In fact, Tom Keating died just a year or so ago. Keating was a notorious forger who used glycerin. His motivation was to prove to the world how he could dupe the experts, which he did, until they tried cleaning the paintings. Keating also used lead white under some of his forgeries, so when they were x-rayed, the white illuminated, thereby revealing his 'time bomb,' as he called it."

Dominic's nostrils flared, as he spat, "That's damn stupid!" He gazed back at his brilliant fake as his mind reeled. "Son of a bitch!" he cussed. "I paid fifty Gs for this piece of shit."

"Ouch!" Bernard said. "Well, if it eases the pain, I lost more than that on a fake Messina, and a few others. It's an ugly part of our business, so get used to it."

Dominic shook his head. "No! I won't. This sucks! It's time for another profession." He grabbed his worthless canvas and headed for the door, as he said without turning, "I'll show myself out."

Bernard looked at Armand. "Well, I'm sorry I dragged you into this. But, as usual, you did an excellent job. I'll cut you a check."

"Hold onto the check," Armand said. "This case isn't over."

"What do you mean?"

"I mean I'm glad I prevented you from buying a fake, Bernie, but I must find this forger. So, I'm off to Rome."

As Armand patted Bernard on the back and started for the door, Higley said, "What's in Rome?"

"Sergio Lavanti."

Two days later, Armand arrived in Rome on Alitalia, rented a car, and drove into the suburbs. Cruising through the Municipio XII sector, he arrived at the Lavanti estate. As he pulled up, he saw trucks being loaded with valuables by three workers, while a young man with a silk sport jacket and white sneakers directed them.

Armand stepped out of the car and approached the young man. "*Ciao*," Armand said in Italian, "*Lei parla inglese?*"

"*Si*, ah, yes," the young man said.

"My name is Armand Arnolfini." He reached out and shook his hand. "I assume you're Sergio Lavanti?"

"Yes," he said. "How can I help you?"

Armand glanced at the beautiful sprawling villa, then at Sergio. "My father knew your uncle. I'm sorry to hear of your loss."

"*Grazie*," Sergio said. "He was a great uncle. My father died ten years ago. Luca was my mentor. I'm the last of the Lavantis, and Uncle Luca wanted to make sure I was wealthy enough to revive the family name, especially since he lost a great deal of money in the stock market over the past two years." He gazed at the cobblestoned pavement, then timidly back up. "I'm an artist, and well…it hasn't been the most profitable past seven years, so he told me to abandon my dream to be the protector of the Lavanti realm, so to speak. The thought of his prized possessions being devoured by the government and our family name vanishing truly vexed him."

Armand's ears had perked up upon hearing that Sergio was an artist. "Well, I wish you luck with your mission. Keeping up an expensive villa like this requires a lot of money." He looked at the men loading the truck, then back at Sergio. "I see they're taking away some of Luca's priceless paintings."

Sergio nodded. "Yes, I'm holding onto the ones I like, but I've been selling quite a few. I'd like to start collecting works by other famous artists, as well as emerging artists struggling to break through. My uncle taught me that many wise entrepreneurs bought up large quantities of works by unknown living artists at dirt cheap prices, banking on them becoming wildly famous, and watched the prices go through the roof. The potential ROI on fine art is a niche market that yields enormous returns, beyond most other commodities, yet few people realize that. You could potentially buy a work for 100 US dollars, and in several years, if that artist strikes it big, get 300,000 dollars, maybe more."

Naturally, Armand already knew that, but he was interested to see if Sergio also intended to make a killing by selling his own forgeries to augment the Lavantis' struggling estate. "Yes, it's a lucrative market, for sure, Sergio." He glanced at the truck. "I believe I saw them load a work by Giovanni Baglione."

Sergio nodded matter-of-factly. "Yeah, it was. The National Gallery in Rome just bought it."

Armand was impressed. "It's a very nice work. I love the Baroque era."

Sergio's face wrinkled like a fig in the sun. "Not me. I don't care for Baroque works. That's why I'm selling those off."

Armand got the conversation where he wanted, and asked, "So, in what genre do *you* paint?"

Sergio smiled. "I paint, what I call Transcendental Abstract-Fusion." He stepped over to his inherited Ferrari, pulled out a tattered portfolio, and brought it over. He opened it up and proudly flipped through the pages, making sure to explain the meaning behind each photo of his incomprehensible paintings.

Armand nodded slowly. "Oh, I see," he said politely, as he struggled to view Sergio's artwork. To Armand, they looked like a series of old discarded palettes with dabs of paint, some thick and textured, while others were mixed smoothly, yet muddy. Armand was utterly convinced— Sergio didn't have the skills to pull off a brilliant fake like the Artemisia. It was now time to reveal his true intention for the visit.

"Very nice, Sergio. But, I'm a private investigator, and I really came here to find out about the Gentileschi painting you sold to Dominic Cafaldo."

"Oh," Sergio said, a bit flustered, expecting Armand to have an interest in his art. "Uh, the Gentileschi, yes, what about it?"

"I'd like to know how that transaction went down. Was that painting in your uncle's collection, or did you recently purchase it yourself?"

Sergio shook his head adamantly. "*Me,* buy it!? No, Mr. Arnolfini. As I told you, I'm looking to unload my uncle's Baroque paintings, not buy them. But, yes, that painting was here, in his villa when I came to assess his entire collection." Sergio closed his portfolio. "Soon after, Dominic contacted me. Evidently, he read my uncle's obituary, which naturally mentioned his prominent art collection. He flew here from New York, and we made the transaction."

Armand nodded thoughtfully. "So, Dominic lives in New York."

"Yes, but he has family here, somewhere in Rome."

"I see. And do you happen to have your uncle's receipt for purchasing the Gentileschi?"

"No. Oddly enough, that's the only painting in my uncle's collection that didn't have a receipt or any paperwork. So, I'm sorry, I can't help you in regards to its provenance."

Armand sighed. That now slammed shut his ability to track down it's origins and it's mysterious creator. "Okay, thank you for your time, Sergio," Armand said glumly, as he handed him his card. "Feel free to call my cell phone number if you ever have problems buying or selling your uncle's artwork."

With that, Armand hopped in his rented car and drove off. As he did, his only recourse flashed across his mind.

Thirty-seven minutes later, Armand arrived at *Carabinieri* headquarters and met his old friend, Salvatore Frangello.

"Sal! Good to see you," Armand said, as they embraced and kissed each other's cheeks.

Salvatore extended Armand backward. "Let me get a good look at you." His eyes scanned Armand from head to toe. "You must be living well, you gained a few pounds."

Armand chuckled. "Yes, life is good, Sal."

"Yes, America and McDonald's can do that."

"No! No! No! I don't touch that stuff," Armand said defensively.

"Ah, of course not, I jest, you always loved good food," Salvatore said. With genuine admiration, he added, "You know that you were my favorite *fútbol* player on AC Milan. *Sì, mio caro amico?*"

"*Si*, Salvatore. *Grazie*. But that was many years ago."

Salvatore sat behind his desk and pointed to a chair. "Sit. So, what brings you here?"

"The Lavanti estate," Armand said, as he sat down. "I know Luca passed away a month ago and his nephew, Sergio, is now selling off some of Luca's art."

"Yes, that is true," Salvatore said. "So, what's the problem?"

"The problem is, one of those pieces happened to be a forgery, which a guy named Dominic Cafaldo tried to sell to a friend of mine at the Cloisters Museum in New York."

"Ah, I see. But, how can *I* help you?"

"This Cafaldo fellow has relatives here in Rome. Before I hunt them down and start asking questions, I'd like to know if there's any criminal records related to the family?"

"Certainly," Salvatore said, as he spun around in his swivel chair and called out, "Peppino! *Vieni qui!*"

As Peppino scurried to his commander's desk, Salvatore said in Italian, "Look up any Cafaldos living in Rome, and give me a full report on any criminal activity."

Peppino nodded dutifully and dashed to the filing cabinet. Meanwhile, Armand and Salvatore caught up on recent endeavors and reminisced about old times. Twenty minutes later, Peppino returned, and said in Italian, "I found only one Cafaldo living in Rome. There's nothing serious, just one excessive speeding ticket, two years ago, and one driving while under the influence. But that was twelve years ago."

"*Grazie*," Salvatore said.

Peppino nodded. "*Prego*," he replied, then returned to his desk.

Salvatore looked at Armand. "Well, this Cafaldo is clean. As far as we know."

"Not so!" another *Carabiniere* said in Italian while walking by. He stopped and approached the desk. "You said Cafaldo. *Si?*"

As Salvatore nodded, he went on, "I received a call yesterday from a young woman, named Carla Belzoni. She claimed to have seen a man, whom she identified as Ricardo Cafaldo, breaking into the Lavanti's garage two weeks ago."

"Two weeks ago?" Salvatore questioned.

"Yes, you see, Carla used to have a relationship with Ricardo, but they recently had a falling out. You know, a woman scorned kind of thing."

Armand interjected in Italian, "Okay, so what exactly did Carla see him do?"

The *Carabiniere* looked at Armand. "She said she saw him bringing, what appeared to be, a painting in to the villa."

Salvatore squinted. "In to, not out of? Are you sure you've got that right, Vincenzo?"

"Yes!" Armand interjected again. "It makes sense."

Vincenzo shook his head. "Not to me, *Senore*, that's why I dragged my feet on investigating her call."

Salvatore added, "Yes, Armand, someone would be *stealing* the valuables from the estate, not adding to them…" Salvatore just realized what he said. "Oh! Wait. Do you think it was—"

"The Gentileschi," Armand cut in. "Yes!" He looked up at Vincenzo. "*Grazie*," he said, then he turned toward Salvatore. "Do you mind if I visit Ricardo first, alone? You can supply backup." He glanced at Vincenzo, then back at Salvatore. "I have a new Motorola cell phone and can call them once they're needed."

Salvatore thought for just a second, then nodded. "*Certamente*," he said. He turned and instructed Vincenzo and Peppino to follow and stay undercover just outside the Cafaldo premises.

Twenty minutes later, Armand arrived at Ricardo's house with a carrying case for his brick cell phone and knocked on the door.

Ricardo Cafaldo answered the door. He was lanky with jet-black hair and in his early thirties. "*Ciao. Come posso aiutarla?* (How can I help you?)"

Armand spoke in Italian: "I'm from New York. I know Dominic Cafaldo. Do you speak English?"

Ricardo's pleasant face wilted. "Yes, please come in."

As Armand entered, he noticed Ricardo's hands had paint on them. "Are you a house painter or an artist?"

"An artist," Ricardo said. "Didn't my cousin tell you?"

"Not exactly. But, I'd love to see what you're working on. I'm an art dealer myself."

Ricardo hesitated, then said, "Fine. Follow me," as he walked down the hallway and entered a rear studio.

Armand followed, and as he entered, he was bathed in sunlight by the string of skylights on the cathedral ceiling. He quickly noticed the stacks of canvases leaning against two walls, some blank and others with various scenes, some surreal, others elaborate landscapes, all painted with the finesse of photo-realism.

Armand then turned and looked at Ricardo's current work, sitting on a large easel. He was taken aback by Ricardo's superb technique, while his creativity of making the painting look as if a large shard of a fresco that had fallen off of a wall was brilliant. Armand also marveled over Ricardo's contemporary use of rich colors, the beauty of the woman's portrait, and his mastery of atmospheric perspective, with the distant mountains having shades of purple and blue with slightly blurred edges due to the moisture in the air, a scientific discovery first recorded and mastered by Leonardo, who explained the technique in detail in his *Treatise on Art*.

Armand stepped closer, examining Ricardo's brushstrokes. "Very, very nice work, Ricardo." He turned around and looked straight into his eyes. "So, why did you do it?"

Ricardo proudly looked at his painting, and said, "Because it's a portrait of my girlfriend gazing at the hills of Rome. She inspires me. It's called *Roman Reveries.*"

Ricardo looked back at Armand, who said, "I'm not referring to *this* painting, Ricardo. I mean the painting of *Judith Beheading Holofernes.*"

Ricardo blinked with a nervous twitch. "W-what makes you say that?" he said, as he tried to suppress his surprise.

"Because I'm an art expert *and* a private investigator, Ricardo. I can see the way you handle paint and the skill you have for realism. Even the Gentileschis would have been proud." Armand glanced at the jar on the table. "And, I see you have glycerin, which we found in your painting. It was very nicely done, I might add. You know, how it washed away the paint, revealing the fake that it was."

Ricardo's shoulders wilted as a wave of humiliation washed over him. "I did it because Dominic forced me to."

"That sounds like a cop out, Ricardo. You're certainly old enough to know better." He glanced back at the stunning canvas. "And you certainly have the talent. This painting is quite beautiful. Yet I imagine this is your *new* girlfriend, not Carla."

Ricardo's eyebrows rose. "How do you know about Carla?"

"Because she phoned the *Carabinieri* yesterday and reported you breaking into the Lavanti estate last month. Evidently, Carla was not too thrilled that you dumped her for another woman."

Ricardo smirked. "I should have known," he uttered, turning his head away in disgust. His head snapped back. "But I didn't cheat on her—*I swear*! I waited until we broke up to start dating Gabriella. Carla just didn't take it very well, and she still stalks me. I'm telling you the truth." Ricardo nervously bit his lips, then added, "And you don't know Dominic. If you did, you'd know he's a low-life drug dealer. He got busted eight years ago for his shady racket, and for beating a rival drug lord almost to death. He spent the last eight years in prison and just recently got released. And he always used to brag about how be bumped off his rivals in his crazy gang wars. So, he's a man to be feared. He's dangerous! And if I didn't listen to him, he threatened to break my hands, to make sure I'd never paint again."

Armand was starting to believe Ricardo's story. He didn't like Dominic the moment he met him, and could imagine him putting the squeeze on his talented cousin. "So, that's why Dominic changed his career, to avoid getting busted with drugs again. Is that it?"

"You got it," Ricardo said through his gritted teeth. "I hate the bastard! I didn't want to do it, I swear. That's why I used materials in the paint that I knew an expert would find. But then I discovered glycerin, which would easily give it away. The plan was to get Dominic arrested and thrown in the slammer for life."

"But what about the blowback? Didn't you realize that this would eventually lead back to you?"

Ricardo nodded. "Yeah, I thought about that, but then realized that art crimes in America aren't taken seriously. We have the most effective art crime squads here in Italy, second to none. But, I figured the Americans would be happy enough putting Dominic away for good, knowing his past criminal record, and drop the art fraud investigation."

He looked sullenly down at the floor, then back up into Armand's eyes. "But I didn't count on someone like *you*!"

Once again, Armand was confronted with a man he initially had contempt for, but upon hearing Ricardo's touching story, he succumbed to feelings of sympathy. Here was a man struggling to make a living as an artist, yet forced into a situation not of his own doing, and made a pawn upon threats of hostility that would cripple him and end his career.

Armand looked at Ricardo. There was still one last question he needed to ask. "But what about the 50,000 dollars Dominic paid you? You did pretty well for yourself."

"Fifty thousand!?" Ricardo blurted scathingly. "That lying dog! He only gave me 50 of your US dollars, which barely covered my paint and canvas." Ricardo grasped a rag, humiliated, and washed the paint off his hands, then threw the rag down. He looked at Armand and extended his arms. "Go ahead! Cuff me. I'm through with this nonsense."

"No," Armand said. "I have no intentions of extraditing you. And I doubt the *Carabinieri* outside will cuff you, especially once I tell them your story. I'm sure they'll prosecute you, but I'll do whatever I can to make them ease the sentencing, perhaps only giving you community service." Armand's eyes veered sideways in thought, then back at Ricardo. "In fact, I think I'll suggest that they have you paint a mural in a public square as punishment." Armand smiled. "That would give you an excellent platform to advertise your work and jumpstart your career."

Ricardo's hunched shoulders sprang upright as a grin enlivened his youthful face. "Would you really do that for me?"

"I wouldn't lie to you, Ricardo. As I always say, 'Lying is a full-time job, one best to quit.'"

Ricardo chuckled. "That's a great quote. I'll have to remember that."

Armand slipped his cell phone out of its case. "I need to call them in now. Are you ready?"

Ricardo nodded. "I'll call Gabriella once I get down to the station. And thank you. You're a good man. I won't let you down, I swear."

"I believe you, Ricardo. The real criminal is Dominic. And I think you did a fine job of luring him into a trap. When I return home, I'll make sure he's picked up. So, I thank you."

With that, Armand called Vincenzo, who soon arrived with Peppino. Armand followed them to the station and explained the entire affair to Salvatore, who assured Armand that his fitting punishment would be presented at the trial and carried out.

The next day Armand arrived at La Guardia Airport and drove straight to the Cloisters Museum, where he met Bernard Higley. Bernard gave Armand Dominic's phone number and address, which Armand relayed over to his friends at the precinct. Within the hour, Dominic Cafaldo was arrested.

A month later, Dominic was convicted of art fraud and racketeering. Added to the charges was the recent discovery of a ten-year-old cadaver with bullets riddled throughout its torso, the bullets matching Dominic's Glock 17, semi-automatic. It was the end result of a drug war gone bad. The judge sentenced Dominic to forty years in Attica Correctional Facility, a maximum-security prison.

Upon hearing this news, Armand walked into the dining room of his home with a bottle of champagne.

Andrea had already taken her seat and looked up as Armand popped the cork. "What's the champagne for?"

Armand smiled. "Because Dominic Cafaldo has been put away, and Ricardo recently finished his mural, which received accolades in the press. A win-win situation."

Andrea clapped. "Bravo! That *is* worth celebrating."

"You know I can only give you a drop to wet your lips, honey. But I want to share this moment with you, as well as with our darling unborn baby."

"Well, we'll have to come up with a name," Andrea said. "Because I got the sonogram results today."

Armand eagerly sat down. "Well!" What is it? A boy or a girl?" he asked as he poured the champagne.

"Well, perhaps you should have asked 'Is it a *girl* or a boy?' You'll have to start being more mindful of women from now on."

Armand's face lit up. "A girl! That's fantastic, sweetheart!" He handed Andrea her flute, with only a few drops of champagne, and lifted his glass. "Well, I said *boy* first because it's a colloquialism. It's been a man's world for many centuries, but we must thank strong women, like Artemisia and countless others, who helped to change our perceptions and expressions."

They clinked glasses, and toasted.

Having swallowed his sip of bubbly, Armand said, "Hey! How about we name her Artemisia?"

Andrea smiled. "Well, isn't Artemisia also the name of a plant?"

"Yes, but so are the names Fern, Rose, Violet and many others."

Andrea nodded. "I guess you're right. And it's certainly unique, that's for sure."

"And when pronounced properly," he said, "Aar·tuh·mee·zhuh rolls off the tongue rather beautifully, even artistically."

Andrea nodded. "Yes, it does. I like it. More importantly, it honors a strong and talented woman."

"Indeed it does," Armand said. "Moreover, it ensures they'll be no amnesia of Artemisia."

As Andrea smiled, Armand rose up, walked over, and warmly embraced his plump, beautiful wife. He kissed her, then returned to his seat. They each picked up their forks and enjoyed a splendid meal of Caesar salad, clams casino, baby lamb chops, and eggplant rollatini, while tender thoughts of their daughter filled their heads. They looked deeply into each other's eyes, knowing that their future was going to be simply radiant, miraculous even. Life was grand.

Artemisia Gentileschi *Self Portrait*

Thank You

Thanks again to all my readers for expressing your enjoyment with the character Armand Arnolfini. The first two episodes had appeared in *Short Stories II: Mysteries, Thrillers & Historical*. It was your support that prompted me to write *The Arnolfini Art Mysteries*, which received a very warm reception. As such, this volume continues the series.

The adventures within take Armand to some new and interesting locations and of course brings to light some fantastic works of art and even architecture. This series enables me to share my love of the creative arts with others, many of whom never had the good fortune to see these magnificent works. And that, in and of itself, makes this series more than mere entertainment, for art truly can lift the soul.

As stated before, I am indebted to all the great artists who have influenced me over the years and made these fictional adventures possible. Their contributions to Western civilization are indeed to be cherished, and I feel couching them in entertaining mysteries brings their names and talents to a broader public not acquainted with their work. In this volume, Artemisia Gentileschi was a special addition, being that women have sadly been overshadowed and marginalized by historians for far too long, and it was a pleasure writing that particular chapter.

To my dear family and friends who have supported my creative endeavors, along with my editors, marketers, and to all the contest judges who have voted several of my books as award winners, I am most grateful

— *Rich DiSilvio*

My Nazi Nemesis

GOLD AWARD WINNER

★★★★★ "DiSilvio's plot is cunning and ingenious!"
-- Jack Magnus for Readers' Favorite

A deadly love triangle launches a father and daughter team to hunt down a nefarious Nazi. Yet twists and turns abound, leading to a shocking climax.

Hardcover: 9780981762586
Paperback: 9780981762579
eBook: 9780981762593

A Blazing Gilded Age

INTERNATIONAL AWARD WINNER AND BEST COVER DESIGN

A riveting rags-to-riches saga about a poor family's struggle to survive amid a nation burning with ambition yet bleeding with injustice. Features, Teddy Roosevelt, JP Morgan, Mark Twain, Tesla and more.

Lauded by HISTORY/A+E and noted biographer Roger DiSilvestro.

Hardcover: 9780981762562
Paperback: 9780981762555
eBook: 9780997680720

Tales of Titans Series

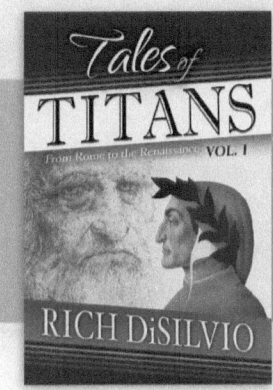 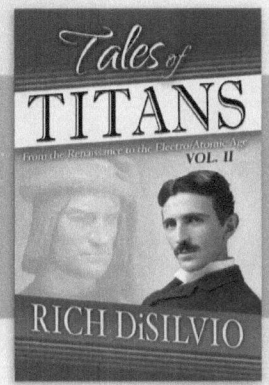 

Tales of Titans brings great historical figures to life with concise yet compelling essays, coupled with engaging narratives that enlighten readers to their miraculous deeds, and misdeeds, that have significantly shaped Western civilization.

This handsomely illustrated series offers readers brief biographical overviews and cogent analysis, while the quasi-fictional scenarios transport readers into a fascinating past, whereby putting flesh on the bones of several titans and offering glimpses into their hearts, minds, and actions.

Tales of Titans, Vol. I : From Rome to the Renaissance
Augustus & Livia, Vespasian & Titus, Hadrian, Constantine, Dante, Brunelleschi, Columbus, Vespucci, King Ferdinand, Pope Alexander VI & Cesare Borgia, and Leonardo da Vinci.

Tales of Titans, Vol. II: Renaissance to the Electro/Atomic Age
The Medicis, Gutenberg, Lorenzo de Medici, Savonarola, Leonardo & Machiavelli, Martin Luther, Queen Elizabeth I, Shakespeare, Galileo, Darwin, Marx, Stalin, Freud, Marconi, Edison, Tesla, Westinghouse, Einstein, Fermi and von Braun.

Tales of Titans, Vol. III: Founding Fathers, Women Warriors & WWII
Samuel Adams, Thomas Paine, George Washington, John Adams, Thomas Jefferson, James Madison, Alexander Hamilton, Ben Franklin, Sybil Ludington, James Armistead Lafayette, Elizabeth Cady Stanton, Susan B. Anthony, Harriet Tubman, Adolf Hitler, FDR & Churchill

Liszt's *Dante Symphony*

A historical mystery/thriller highlighting the belligerent rise of Nazi Germany from its Prussian roots, replete with ciphers, spies, murder and a stellar cast, including Albert Einstein, Rossini, Liszt, Nazi officers and Adolf Hitler.

Hardcover: 9780981762548
Paperback: 9780981762531
eBook: 9780997680713

The Winds of Time

The Winds of Time is a historical tour de force of Western civilization by Rich DiSilvio.

With masterful style, DiSilvio paints a fascinating historical canvas with the flare of a consummate artist. Key figures and the primary cultures that literally shaped the Western world are candidly analyzed, revealing both the dark and luminous sides of mankind. Moreover, DiSilvio's insightful essays add intriguing new dimensions to the historical record.

Hardcover: 9780981762524
eBook: 9780997680706

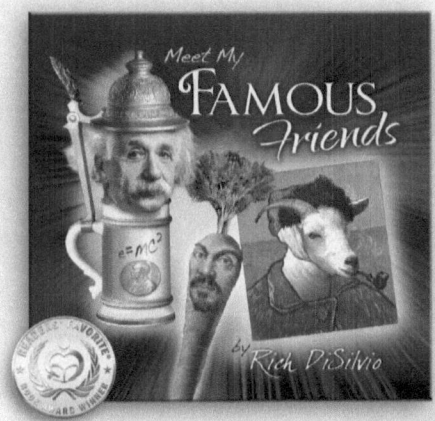

SILVER MEDAL WINNER
Meet My Famous Friends

Inspiring kids with Humor!
A whimsical picture book that pays homage to great historical figures in imaginative ways.

Author/Illustrator Rich DiSilvio presents a broad array of geniuses and heroes in a humorous and compelling fashion by altering their names and appearances, whereby making us see very familiar people in very different ways.

While children will get a kick out of looking at the comical artwork, teens and even adults will appreciate the witty play on words, inventive creations, and perhaps glean a thing or two about some of these iconic people who had a great influence on society in one form or another. Their lives and contributions have uplifted humanity in various ways, thus being great role models for young and old alike.

Hardcover: 9780997680751 Paperback: 9780997680768 eBook: 9780997680775

PURPLE DRAGONFLY WINNER
Danny and the DreamWeaver

A MS novelette by Mark Poe (aka Rich DiSilvio) about the power of dreams and the imagination.

When Danny meets Nostrildamus in his dream a bizarre journey begins!

Packed with dry humor, a mystery, and zany-looking artists, like Michelanjello & Hippopotamus Bosch, *Danny and the DreamWeaver* is an imaginative adventure of criminal intrigue and art history that demonstrates the importance of looking at life differently.

Paperback: 9780997680737
eBook: 9780997680744

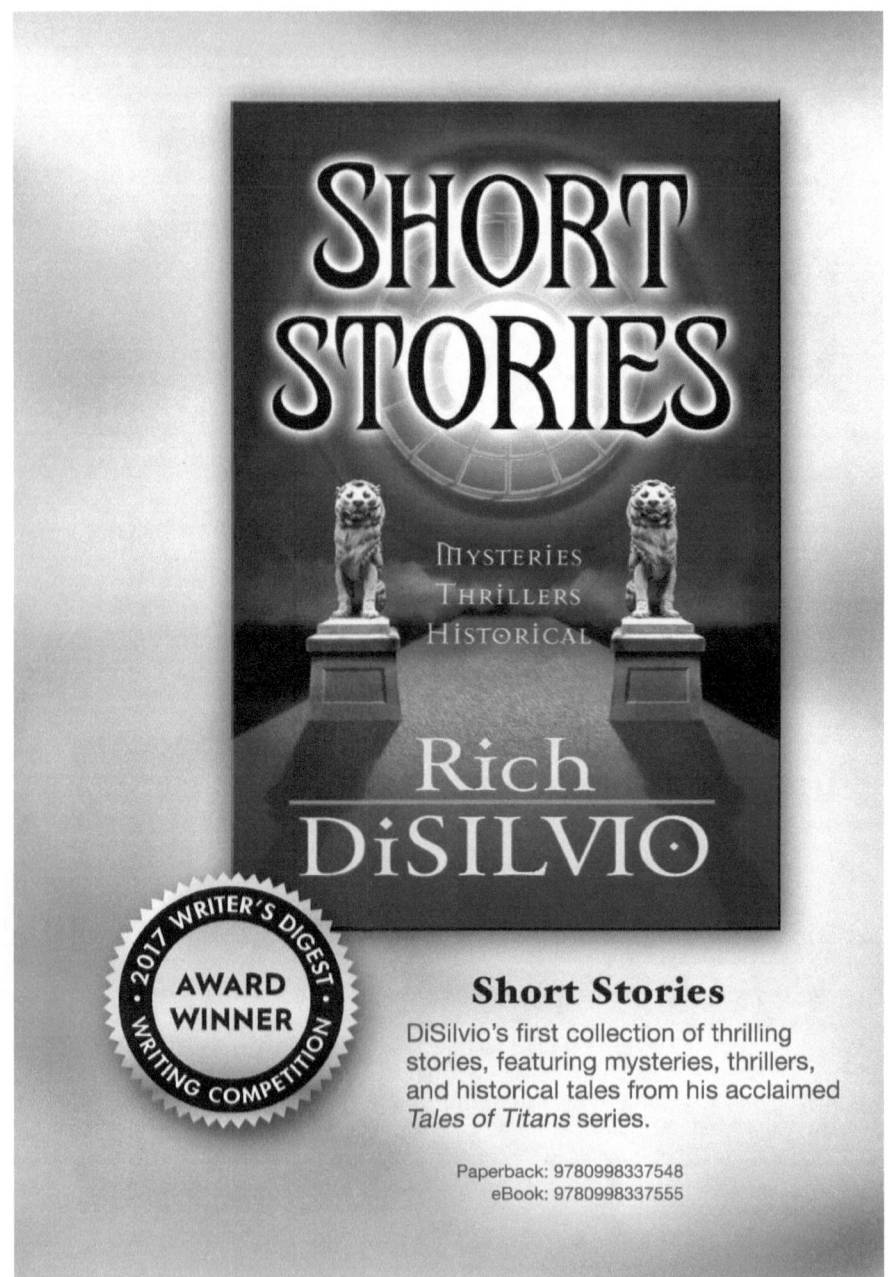

Short Stories

DiSilvio's first collection of thrilling stories, featuring mysteries, thrillers, and historical tales from his acclaimed *Tales of Titans* series.

Paperback: 9780998337548
eBook: 9780998337555

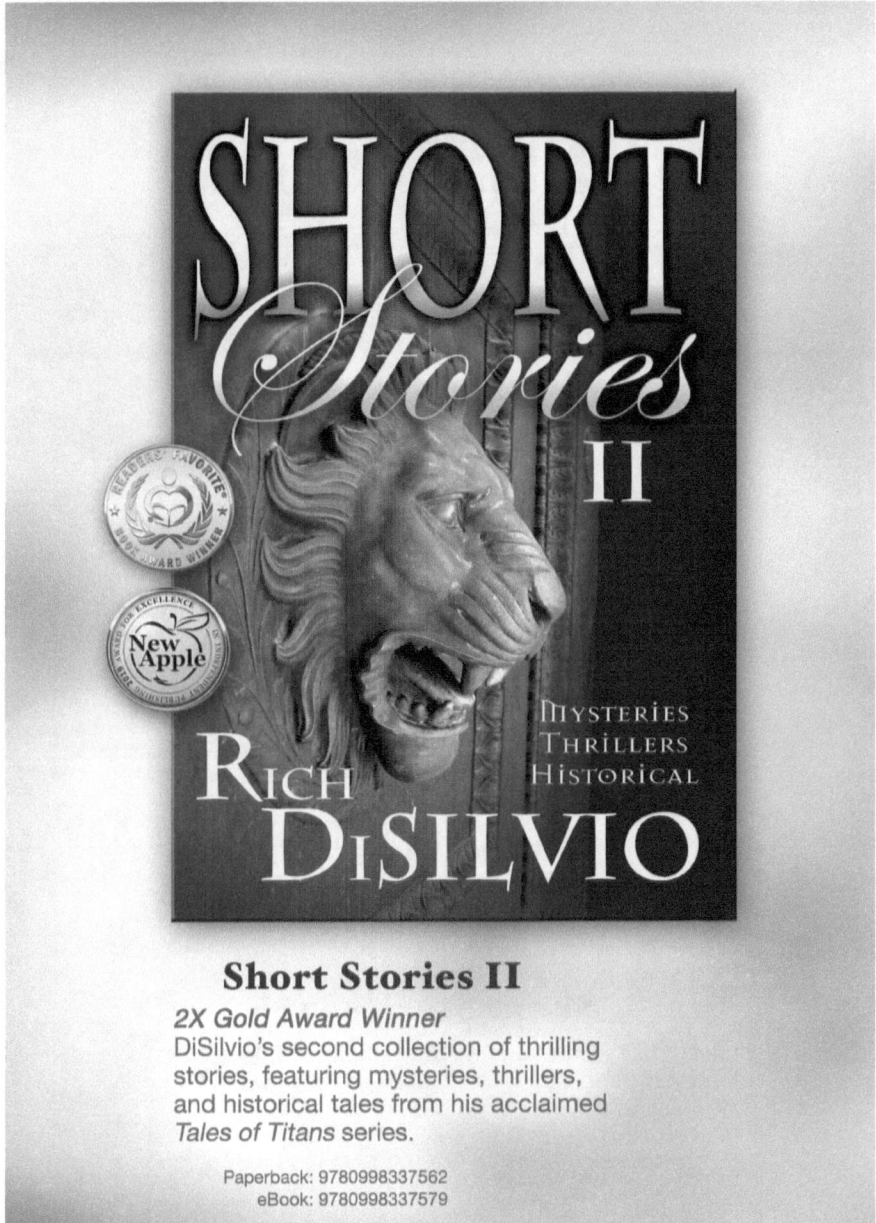

Short Stories II

2X Gold Award Winner
DiSilvio's second collection of thrilling stories, featuring mysteries, thrillers, and historical tales from his acclaimed *Tales of Titans* series.

Paperback: 9780998337562
eBook: 9780998337579

Short Stories III

From the vivid imagination of multi-award-winning author/artist Rich DiSilvio comes this spellbinding collection of fantasy and Sci-Fi tales.

Paperback: 9780998337586
eBook: 9780998337593

Short Stories IV

From the vivid imagination of multi-award-winning
author/artist Rich DiSilvio comes this spellbinding
second collection of fantasy and Sci-Fi tales.

Paperback: 9781950052004
eBook: 9781950052011

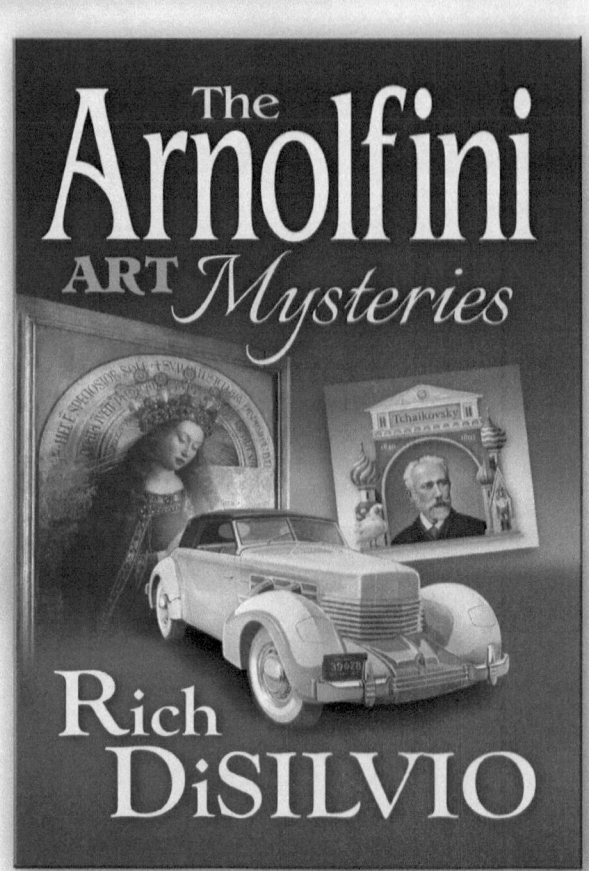

The Arnolfini Art Mysteries

The first volume featuring the intriguing adventures of Armand Arnolfini, the charismatic and clever private eye who hunts down crafty art forgers, unscrupulous thieves and ruthless murderers.

Hardciver: 978-1-950052-04-2
Paperback: 978-1-950052-02-8
eBook: 978-1-950052-03-5

NOTE TO THE READER

For those not acquainted with fine art or architecture, I feel it's my duty to inform you of the speculative revisions of history contained in several cases.

In *Leonardo's Leda*, please note that da Vinci's long-lost painting has regrettably never been found. As indicated in the story, it was last seen in 1625 at the Château de Fontainebleau by Cassiano dal Pozzo.

In *The Carpeaux Caper*, please note that the sculptor never drew plans for a *Liszt Monument*. Nor did he sculpt a bust of Franz Liszt. However, Carpeaux did sculpt busts of the French composer Charles Gounod and French artist Jean Gérôme, as mentioned.

In the *Five and Dime Mystery*, no architectural plans were found in the gargoylesque statue of Cass Gilbert, and while Giuseppe Mengoni did fall off the roof of the *Galleria* to his death, he was not pushed, as Carlo Giancotta is a fictional character.

I am happy to report that Artemisia and her father Orazio did exist, and highlighting their works was a pleasure, especially those of Artemisia's, which deserve far more recognition than history has allotted. Meanwhile, the painting *Roman Reveries* by the fictional character Ricardo Cafaldo was by your host—Rich DiSilvio.

www.ingramcontent.com/pod-product-compliance
Lightning Source LLC
Chambersburg PA
CBHW032003240626
47153CB00003B/1102